ST. PATRICK

FOR

IRELAND.

ST. PATRICK FOR IRELAND.] This singular drama is another of those which Shirley gave to the Dublin theatre. In the title to the old copy, printed in 1640, it is called the *First Part ;* but it does not appear that a *Second* was ever produced, though conditionally promised in the Prologue ; this in all probability was owing to the Poet's return to England on the decline of the Earl of Strafford's power. The play is not among those licensed by the Master of the Revels.

The events on which the plot is built, may be found in Bede, and other early historians, and in the *Life of St. Patrick.*

PROLOGUE.

We know not what will take ; your palates are
Various, and many of them sick, I fear :
We can but serve up what our poets dress ;
And not considering cost, or pains to please,
We should be very happy if, at last,
We could find out the humour of your taste,
That we might fit, and feast it, so that you
Were constant to yourselves, and kept that true ;
For some have their opinions so diseas'd,[1]
They come not with a purpose to be pleas'd :
Or, like some birds that leave the flow'ry fields,
They only stoop at that corruption yields.
It were a custom would less stain the times,
To praise the virtues, when you chide the crimes:
This is but cold encouragement ; but we
Hope here are few of those ; or, if there be,
We wish them not infectious : nor confine
We censures ; would each soul were masculine !
For your own sakes, we wish all here to-day
Knew but the art and labour of a play ;
Then you would value the true muses' pain,
The throes and travail of a teeming brain.
But we have no despair, that all here may
Be friends, and come with candour to this play,
St. Patrick, whose large story cannot be
Bound in the limits of one play, if ye
First welcome this, you'll grace our poet's art,
And give him courage for a Second Part.

---

[1] For *diseas'd*, the old copy reads *displeas'd*.

DRAMATIS PERSONÆ.

Leogarius, *king of* Ireland.
Corybreus, } *his sons.*
Conallus,
Dichu, *a nobleman.*
Ferochus, } *his sons.*
Endarius,
Milcho, *a great officer.*
Archimagus, *the chief priest, a magician.*
Two other Magicians.
St. Patrick.
Victor, *his angelic guardian.*
Rodamant, Archimagus' *servant.*
Bard.
Soldiers.
Angels.
Priests, followers of St. Patrick.
Servants.
Spirits.
Serpents, &c.

Queen.
Ethne, } *her daughters.*
Fedella,
Emeria, Milcho's *daughter.*

SCENE, *a Temple ; the Royal Residence ; and its vicinity.*

3

ST. PATRICK FOR IRELAND.

ACT I. SCENE I.

The Temple, with statues of Jupiter and Saturn; in front an altar.

Enter ARCHIMAGUS *with a scroll, and two other* Magicians, *at several doors.*

1 Mag. We are undone.
2 Mag. We are lost.
Arch. Not so; your fears
Become you not, great priests of Jove and Saturn.
Shall we, that awe the Furies, at whose charm
Hell itself quakes, be frighted with a shadow?
A tame, a naked churchman, and his tribe
Of austere, starved faces? No; this kingdom
Shall still be our's, and flourish; every altar
Breathe incense to our gods, and shine with flames,
To strike this Christian blind.
1 Mag. This is but air:
He is now landing; every tread he prints
Upon this earth will make it groan.
Arch. Are not
The havens strengthen'd, by the king's command,
With soldiers, to watch that none arrive
With this suspicion?[1]
2 Mag. But we, that can

---

[1] *With this suspicion ?*] Meaning, perhaps, suspected of being a Christian; but the expression is so awkward that its genuineness may be doubted.

4

Command armies from hell for our design,
And blast him, now stand idle, and benumb'd ;
And shall grow here ridiculous statues.   I'll
Muster my fiends.^a
  1 *Mag.* And if I have not lost
My power, the spirits shall obey, to drown
This straggler, and secure this threaten'd island.
   Arch. Stay ! Which of you can boast more power
      than I ?
For every spirit you command, my spells
Can raise a legion ; you know I can
Untenant hell, dispeople the wide air,
Where, like innumerous atoms, the black genii
Hover, and jostle one another.   All
That haunt the woods and waters, all i' the dark
And solitary chambers of the earth,
Break through their adamantine chains, and fly,
Like lightning, to my will ; and shall your factious
And petty correspondence with the fiends
Attempt this work without my voice and counsel ?
Who brought you first acquainted with the devil ?
Did not my art?
  1 *Mag.* We are disciples to
The great Archimagus.
  2 *Mag.* We acknowledge all
Our art derived from you.
  1 *Mag.* But in this justice to our gods, we hope
Our gods' chief priest will give us leave—
   Arch. Yes, and confirm it, and applaud your zeal,
My fellows both in sacred arts and priesthood :
Go on, I praise your resolution.
My spirit gave intelligence before
Of his approach ; and by all circumstance,
Our prophesy doth point this Christian priest
The black subversion of our isle ; but we,
Like masters of all destiny, will break

---

  ^a *Muster my* fiends.] The 4to. reads, *friends:* just below we
have *nistle* for *jostle,* or some similar expression.

5

His fate, and bruise him in his infancy
Of danger to this kingdom.   Fly! and be
Arm'd to your wishes ; spirits shall attend you,
And the whole power of hell.— [*Exe. Magicians.*
This news affrights me,
Howe'er I seem to swell with confidence.
This is the man, and this the revolution,
Fix'd for the change of sacrifice, foretold,
And threatened in this fatal prophesy :   [*Reads.*

> *A man shall come into this land*
> *With shaven crown, and in his hand*
> *A crooked staff ; he shall command,*
> *And in the east his table stand :*
> *From his warm lips a stream shall flow,*
> *To make rocks melt, and churches grow,*
> *Where, while he sings, our gods shall bow,*
> *And all our kings his law allow.*

This, this is the vexation.

Enter ENDARIUS.

End. Sir, the king—
Arch. What of the king ?
End. Is troubled, sick, distracted.
Arch. How ?
End. With a dream ; he has no peace within
    him :
You must with all haste visit him, we shall
Suspect his death else.

Enter FEROCHUS.

Fer. Mighty priest, as you
Respect the safety of the king, you must
Make haste ; the court is up in arms, and he
Calls for his sword.
    Arch. You fright me, gentlemen :
Rebellion in the court ! who are the traitors ?

Fer. His own wild thoughts, and apprehension
Of what, he says, was in his sleep presented.
He calls upon his guard, and rails upon them,
When they appear with no more arms, and swears
That every man shall wear a tun of iron.

Enter CONALLUS.

End. The prince.
Con The king, impatient of your absence, sir,
Hath left the court, and by some few attended,
Is coming hither, laden with fear and weapons;
He talks of strange things in his dream, and frights
Our ears with an invasion, that his crown
Sits trembling on his head. Unless your wisdom
Clear his dark fears, we are undone,
Arch. He's here.—

Enter King, CORYBREUS, *and* DICHU.

How fares the king?
King. Dear Archimagus,
We want thy skill to interpret a black dream
I had last night; my fancy is still sick on't,
And with the very apprehension
I feel much of my soul dissolve, and through
My frighted pores, creep from me in a sweat:
I shall have nothing in me but a bath,
Unless thou do repair my languishing essence
With thy great art and counsel.
Arch. Give me, sir,
The particular of your dream.
King. They must not hear it.
Yet stay; the eclipse, if it be any thing,
Is universal, and doth darken all.—
Methought, Archimagus, as I was praying
I' the temple near the sea, my queen, my sons,
Daughters, and train of my nobility,

7

Prostrate before the altar, on the sudden
The roof did open, and from heaven a flame
Descending on the images of our gods,
Began to burn the sacred brows; from which
Many deformed worms, and hideous serpents
Came crawling forth, and leap'd unto our throats,
Where, with their horrid circles and embrace,
We were almost strangled; in this fright, me-
     thought
We fled out of the temple, and as soon
We saw a pale man coming from the sea,
Attended by a tribe of reverend men,
At whose approach the serpents all unchain'd
Themselves, and leaving our imprison'd necks,
Crept into the earth : straight all that were with me,
As I had been the prodigy, forsook me,
My wife, my children, lords, my servants all,
And fled to this pale man, who told me I
Must submit too, humble myself to him,
This wither'd piece of man ! at which, methought,
I felt a trembling shoot through every part,
And with the horror thus to be depos'd,
I wakened.   Now, Archimagus, thy art,
To cure thy soul-sick king.
   Arch. 'Tis done already.
   King. How, my dear priest ?
   Arch. This pale thing shall not trouble you.
He that so long was threatened to destroy
Us and our gods, is come.
   King. Ha! where ?
   Arch. Now landing ;
But were the coasts unguarded, he wants power
To fight with those ethereal troops, that wait
Upon the gods we serve.   He is now dying,
This minute they have blasted him; and they,
Above the speed of wings, are flying hither
With the glad news.   Be calm again, and let not
These airy dreams distract your peace.

King. They are vanish'd
Already at thy voice; thou, next our gods,
The hope of this great island, hast dispers'd
All clouds, and made it a fair sky again.
My learned Archimagus.

Spirits *are heard.*

1 *Spi.* He is come.
2 *Spi.* He is come.
3 *Spi.* And we must fly.
King. What voices make the air
So sad?
Cor. They strike a horror.
Con. They are spirits.
Arch. I command [you]
Once more to oppose him.
1 *Spi.* In vain, great priest.
2 *Spi.* We must away.
3 *Spi.* Away!
Omnes. We cannot, dare not stay.

Enter Victor, *bearing a banner with a cross,
followed by St.* Patrick, *and other Priests in
procession, singing.*

King. What harmony is this? I have no power
To do them harm. Observe their ceremony.

Ode.

*Post maris sævi fremitus Iërnæ
(Navitas cœlo tremulos beante)
Vidimus gratum jubar enatantes
             Littus inaurans.*

*Montium quin vos juga, vosque sylvæ
Nunc salutamus, chorus advenarum
Jubilum retrò modulantur, ecce
             Carbasa ventis.*

Dulce supremo melos occinamus
Carminum flagrans Domino litamen,
Cujus erranti dabitur popello
              Numine sacrum.

King. I'll speak to him.—Stay! you that have
    presum'd,
Without our leave, to print your desperate foot
Upon our country; say, what bold design
Hath arm'd you with this insolent noise, to dare
And fright the holy peace of this fair isle?
Nay, in contempt of all our gods, advance
Your songs in honour of an unknown Power?
The king commands you speak.
    St. P. Unto that title
Thus we all bow; it speaks you are allied
To heaven, great sir: we come not to distract
Your peace; look on our number; we bring no
Signs of stern war, no invasive force, to draw
Fear or suspicion, or your frowns upon us.
A handful of poor naked men we are,
Thrown on your coast, whose arms are only prayer
That you would not be more unmerciful
Than the rough seas, since they have let us live
To find your charity.
    King. Whence are you?
    St. P. We are of Britain, sir.
    King. Your name, that answer for the rest so
    boldly?
    St. P. My name is Patrick; who, with these
    poor men,
Beseech you would permit—
    King. No dwelling here;
And therefore quit this kingdom speedily,
Or you shall curse you saw the land.
    Dic. Are they not spies?
    Arch. A whirlwind snatch them hence! and on
    the back

Of his black wings transport these fugitives,
And drop their cursed heads into the sea,
Or land them in some cold remotest wilderness
Of all the world! They must not here inhabit.
   Dic. Hence! or we'll force you with these
      goads.
   Cor. Unless
You have a mind to try how well your hoods
Can swim, go trudge back to your rotten bark,
And steer another course.
   Fer. You will find islands
Peopled with squirrels, rats, and crows, and
      coneys,
Where you may better plant, my reverend moles.
   End. Faces about!
   St. P. You are inhospitable,
And have more flinty bosoms than the rocks
That bind your shores, and circle your fair island.
But I must not return.
   King. How!
   Arch. How!
   St. P. Till I have
Perform'd my duty.—Know, great king, I have
Commission for my stay. I came not hither
Without command, legate from Him, before
Whose angry breath the rocks do break and thaw;
To whose nod the mountains humble their proud
      heads.
The earth, the water, air, and heaven is his,
And all the stars that shine with evening flames,
Shew but their trembling when they wait on him:
This supreme King's command I have obey'd,
Who sent me hither to bring you to him,
And this still wand'ring nation, to those springs
Where souls are everlastingly refresh'd;
Unto those gardens, whose immortal flowers
Stain your imagin'd shades, and blest abodes.
   King. What place is this?

St. P. Heaven ; now a great way off ;
But not accessible to those permit
Their precious souls be strangled thus with mists,
And false opinion of their gods.
   Arch. No more.
   St. P. I must say more in my great master's
      cause,
And tell you, in my dreams he hath made me hear,
From the dark wombs of mothers, prison'd infants
Confessing how their parents are misled,
And calling me thus far to be their freedom.
Have pity on yourselves ; be men, and let not
A blind devotion to your painted gods—
   Dic. He does blaspheme. Accept me, Jove,
      thy priest,
And this my sacrifice. [*offers to strike St. P. with
      his spear.*]—Ha ! mine arms grow stiff ;
I feel an ice creeping throngh all my blood ;
There's winter in my heart ; I change o' the sudden,
Am grown a statue, every limb is marble.
Ye gods, take pity on me! in your cause
I wither thus ; Jove, if thou hast a lightning,
Bestow some here, and warm me.
   Cor. Strange!
   End. Father ! Brother, if he should die now ?
   Fer. I am his eldest son, he shall find me rea-
      sonable ;
He may do worse, considering how long
I have been of age.
   Dic. No power let fall compassion ? I have
Offended ; whom, I know not ; this good man.
Forgive, and if the Deity thou serv'st
Can put a life into this frozen pile,
Pray for me.
   King. Villain ! wouldst thou owe thy life
To the mercy of the Power he serves?
   Arch. Wish rather,
To rot for ever thus.

C c 2

King. And if thou diest,
I'll build a temple here, and in this posture
Kings shall kneel to thee, and on solemn days
Present their crowns; queens shall compose thee
    garlands,
Virgins shall sing thy name, and 'bout thy neck
And arms disperse the riches of their art:
Next to our gods we['ll] honour thee.—Keep from
The impostor!
    Cor. I have no meaning to come near him.
    St. P. Give me thy hand. Now, move, and may
    thy heart
Find softness too; this mercy is the least
Of my great master's treasures.
    Dic. I feel my heat
Return'd, and all my rocky parts grow supple.
Let the first use I make of their restore, be
To bend my knees to you.   [*Kneels.*
    St. P. Bow them to him
That gave me power to help thee.
    Fer. He is well again!
    Dic. I find a beam let into my dark soul.
Oh, take me to your faith; here I give back
Myself, to serve your God.
    King. Trait'rous to heaven!
Come from him.
    Dic. Bid me forsake a blessing!
    End. Father!
    Dic. Call this good man your father, boys.
    Arch. He's mad,
And I am frantic at this base apostasy.—
My lord, think how you may provoke our gods,
And the king's anger.
    St. P. Fear his wrath that made,
And can let fall, the world.
    Fer. He may yet do me as great a courtesy
As dying comes to, if his error bold,
And the king's anger.

King. Dotard!
Return, and prostrate to the gods we worship,
Or, though his witchcraft now protect thyself,
Thy sons shall bleed.
   Fer. How's that?
   King. To satisfy
The gods and us, with the next morning's sun,
Unless thou rise, and sacrifice to our altars,
Down from that rock which overlooks the sea,
They shall be thrown; my vow is fix'd.
   Fer. Dear father!
   King. Take them away; their fate depends on him.
   Dic. Oh! I am lost.
   St. P. Thou art found.
   Dic. Forsake me not.—
Poor boys! my prayers and blessing.   [*Rises.*
   St. P. Set forward now, in heaven's name,
And finish our procession.
                    [*Exeunt Dic. St. P. and Priests.*
   King. Death pursue them!
Will nothing make them feel our wrath?
   Cor. The charm
Will not last always.
   Arch. Their fate is not yet ripe.
Be not dejected, sir; the gods cannot
Be patient long; meantime, let me advise,
Not by your laws, or other open force,
To persecute them; but disguise your anger.
   King. Ha!
   Arch. What matter is it, so we destroy these
         wretches,
What ways we take?   Invite him to your court,
Pretend I know not what desires to hear
More of his faith; that you find turns within
Your heart, and tremble at the miracle
Wrought upon Dichu; when he's in your posses-
         sion,
A thousand stratagems may be thought upon,

14

To send his giddy soul most quaintly off to
That fine fantastical reward he dreams on,
I' the 'tother world.

King. Thou hast pleas'd us, Archimagus.

Cor. Great Ceanerachius has inspired the priest!
This is the only way.

Con. I do not like it.

King. It shall be so; he shall be thus invited;
And we will meet him with our queen and daugh-
    ters,
Who shall compose themselves to entertain him.

Arch. Leave me to instruct my princely charge,
    your daughters.

King. Be still their blest director; to thy charge
We gave them up long since; but do not tell them
What happen'd to the apostate Dichu. Women
Have soluble and easy hearts; that accident
May startle their religion: keep them firm
In the devotion to our gods, whose virgins
We hope to call them shortly, if their zeal
Maintain that holy flame that yet hath fill'd
Their bosoms.

Arch. They are the darlings of the temple.

King. Conallus, you shall be the messenger,
And bear our invitation.

Arch. Trouble not
The prince; impose that business on my care.

King. Be it so.

Con. I am glad I am off the employment.

King. All ways to serve our gods are free, and
    good;
When shed for them, they take delight in blood.

                              [*Exeunt.*

15

ACT II. SCENE I.

The Palace Garden.

ETHNE *and* FEDELLA, *dancing.*

Eth. I am weary, and yet I would have more;
my heart
Was never more dispos'd to mirth, Fedella.

Fed. Mine is as light as your's, sister; I am
All air, methinks.

Eth. And I all mounting fire.

Fed. 'Tis well we are alone.

Eth. 'Tis ill we are;
This heat our servants should have given us.

Fed. I wonder we cannot see them; they were
not,
Since we first took them to our favour, guilty
Of such neglect.

Eth. You wrong our birth and blood,
To think they dare neglect us; for if they
Forget what we deserve in loving them,
They owe more duty, as we are the king's
Daughters, than to displease us so.

Fed. That binds
But form and heartless ceremony, sister.
By your favour, I had rather hold my servant
By his own love, that chains his heart to mine,
Than all the bands of state.

Eth. I am of thy mind too.
Would they were here! I shall be sad again.
Fie! what a thing
'Tis for two ladies to be in love, and alone
Without a man so long!

Enter RODAMANT, *with a book.*

Fed. Here's one!

Eth. A foolish one,
Our governor's servant.—How now, Rodamant?

Rod. Keep off!

Fed. What, is the fellow conjuring?

Rod. I would, but I cannot read these devilish names.

Eth. How long hast thou serv'd Archimagus?

Rod. Long enough to have had a devil of mine own, if he had pleased. I have drudged under him almost these seven years, in hope to learn the trade of magic ; and none of his spirits will obey me. Would I were a witch, then I should have a familiar, a sucking devil, upon occasion, to do me service.

Fed. A devil?

Rod. Oh, I lov'd him of a child.

Eth. What wouldst thou do with the devil?

Rod. Only exercise my body ; take the air now and then over steeples, and sail once a month to Scotland in a sieve, to see my friends. I have a grannam there, if I had been ruled, would not have seen me wanted a devil at these years. Pray, madam, speak to my master for me, that my friends may not laugh at me, when I come out of my time ; he has spirits enough : I desire none of his grandees ; a little don Diego Diabolo would serve my turn, if he have but skill in love or physic.

Fed. Physic! for what? art sick?

Rod. I am not sick, but I am troubled with a desperate consumption.

Eth. How ?

Fed. Why, that's nothing—

Rod. To you that are great ladies, and feed high ;

but to a man that is kept lean and hungry, a little falling of the flesh is seen.

Eth. I heard thee name love ; prithee, art thou in love ?

Rod. In love ? look on my sore eyes.

Eth. They are well enough, an thou canst see.

Rod. Yes, I can see a little with them ; would they were out !

Eth. How ! out ?

Rod. Out of their pain. I have but seven teeth and a half, and four of them are rotten. Here's a stump a pick-axe cannot dig out of my gums.

Fed. Are these signs of love ?

Rod. Oh, infallible ; beside, I cannot sleep for dreaming of my mistress.

Eth. So ! and what's her name ?

Rod. You shall pardon me, she is—

Eth. A man, or a woman ?

Rod. Nay, she is a woman, as sure as you are the queen's daughters. I name nobody ; do not you say 'tis the queen ; I am what I am, and she is what she is.

Eth. Well said.

Rod. And if I live, I will die for her : but I forget myself, I had a message to tell you ; first, my master commends him to your graces, and will be here presently ; secondly, I have news. Do you know what I mean ?

Fed. Not we.

Rod. Why then, my lord Ferochus, and his brother Endarius—you know them ?

Eth. What of them ?

Rod. And they know you.

Fed. To the purpose.

Rod. I know not that ; but they are—

Eth. What ?

Rod. Not made for worm's-meat.

Fed. What means the fellow ?

Rod. The king has commanded they shall be thrown from a rock into the sea, that's all. But here's my master, can tell you the whole story.

[*Exit.*

Eth. What said the screech-owl ?

Enter ARCHIMAGUS, *with letters.*

Fed. We hope
Archimagus brings better news ; and yet
His face is cast into a form of sorrow.
What are these ?

Arch. Read, and collect
Your noble forces up ; you will be lost else.—

[*Gives them the letters.*

Alas, poor ladies !
How soon their blood is frighted !

Eth. Every character
Gives my poor heart a wound.

Fed. Alas ! how much of mischief is contain'd
In this poor narrow paper !

Eth. Can this be ?

Arch. Madam, too true ; the anger of the king
Is heavy and inevitable. You may
Believe what their sad pens have bled to you ;
They have no hope, not once before they die,
To see your blessed eyes, and take their leave,
And weep into your bosom their last farewell.

Fed. They must not, shall not die so.

Arch. They must, madam.

Eth. I will die with them too then.—Sister, shall
They leave the world without our company ?

Fed. Could not you bend the king, our cruel
    father ?
You should have said, we lov'd them ; you have most
Power to prevail with him ; you should have told
    him,

19

The gods would be offended, and revenge
Their death with some strange curse upon this island.
   Eth. You knew our loves, and all our meetings,
      sir :
They were not without you ; nor will we live
Without them, tell our father. Did our hearts
Flatter themselves with mirth, to be struck dead
With this, this murdering news ! I'll to the king.
   Arch. Stay, and contain yourselves ; your loves
      are brave,
Nor shall your flame die thus ; as I was first
Of counsel with your thoughts, I will preserve
      them :
They shall not die, if my brain leave me not.
   Fed. Oh, I could dwell upon his lips to thank
      him.
   Arch. But they must then be banished.
   Eth. That's death,
Unless we go along to exile with them.
   Arch. I have the way; they shall deceive the
      sentence
Of the enraged king, and live ; nor shall
This be [the sole] reward of your affections :
You shall converse more often, and more freely
Than ever, if you dare be wise and secret.
   Fed. You make us happy.
   Arch. Here's your elder brother.
Away, and trust to me.   [*Exeunt Fed. and Eth.*

Enter CORYBREUS.

   Cor. Health to our priest !
   Arch. And to your highness.

Enter behind EMERIA *and* CONALLUS.

Do you see that couple ?
   Cor. My brother, and the fair Emeria !

Out of their way; but so to reach their voice :
This place i' the garden's apt.
   Arch. Observe them.   [*Cor. and Arch. retire.*
   Em. But will you not, my lord, repent to have
     placed
Your love so much unworthily?
   Con. Oh, never,
My best Emeria! thou hast a wealth
In thy own virtue above all the world:
Be constant, and I'm blest.
   Em. This hand, and heaven,
Be witness where my heart goes.
   Cor. If my fate
Cannot enjoy thy love, I shall grieve both
Your destinies.
   Arch. Be confident you shall
Enjoy her, if you'll follow my directions.
   Cor. Thou art my genius ; but she's very holy,
And, I fear, too religious to her vows ;
She is devoted much to Ceanerachius,
Head of the gods.
   Arch. Sir, her piety
Prepares your conquest, as I'll manage things.
I will not trust the air too much.
   Con. This kiss, and all's confirm'd.
                    [*Kisses her.*

   Em. Pray, my lord, use
My poor heart kindly, for you take it with you.
   Con. I leave mine in exchange.   [*Exit.*
   Arch. He is gone.   Advance
To your mistress ; and if you want art to move her,
I shall not, sir, to make you prosper ; 'tis
Firmly design'd.   When we meet next, you shall
Know more.   [*Exit.— Cor. comes forward.*
   Cor. How now, my fair Emeria?
   Em. I do beseech your highness' pardon ; I
Did think I was alone.
   Cor. Alone you are

In beauty, sweet Emeria, and all
The graces of your sex.
   Em. You are too great
To flatter me ; and yet this language comes
So near the wickedness of court praise, I dare not
With modesty imagine your heart means so.
   Cor. Yet, in this garden, when you seem'd most
      solitary,
Madam, you had many fair and sweet companions.
   Em. Not I, sir.
   Cor. Yes, and my rivals too, Emeria ;
And now they court thy beauty in my presence,
Proud erring things of nature !   Dost not see,
As thou dost move, how every amorous plant
Doth bow his leavy head, and beckon thee ?
The wind doth practise dalliance with thy hairs,
And weave a thousand pretty nets within
To catch itself.   That violet droop'd but now,
Now 'tis exalted at thy smile, and spreads
A virgin bosom to thee.   There's a rose
Would have slept still within its bud, but at
Thy presence it doth open its thin curtains,
And with warm apprehension looking forth,
Betrays its love in blushes : and that woodbine,
As it would be divorced from the sweet-brier,
Courts thee to an embrace.   It is not dew,
That, like so many pearls, embroiders all
The flowers, but tears of their complaint, with fear
To lose thee, from whose eye they take in all
That makes them beautiful, and with humble necks
Pay duty unto thee, their only spring.
   Em. Your grace is courtly.
   Cor. When these dull vegetals
Shew their ambition to be thine, Emeria,
How much should we, that have an active soul
To know and value thee, be taken with
This beauty ! yet, if you dare trust me, madam,
There's none within the throng of your admirers

More willing, more devote to be your servant,
Than Corybreus.
  Em. I must again beseech
Your pardon, and declare myself most ignorant.
Pray speak your meaning in a dialect
I understand.
  Cor. Why, I do love you, madam.
  Em. If this be it, I dare not, sir, believe
You condescend so low, to love Emeria,
A worthless thing.
  Cor. Why not? I love you, madam.
If there be difference of our birth or state,
When we are compared, it should make me the
     first
In your fair thoughts. Come, you must love again,
And meet me with an equal, active flame.
  Em. I am more skill'd in duty, sir, than love.
  Cor. You would be coy; your heart is not be-
     stow'd?
  Em. Indeed it is.
  Cor. On whom?
  Em. I must not name.
  Cor. Were he my brother did twist heart with
     thine,
That act should make him strange[r] to my blood,
And I would cut him from his bold embraces.
  Em. Alas, I fear.   [*Aside.*
  Cor. I know you will be wise,
And just to my desires, Emeria,
When you shall see my love bid fairest for you,
And that presented from a prince, who knows
No equal here. Come, I already promise
Myself possess'd of those fair eyes, in which
I, gazing thus, at every search discover
New crystal heavens; those tempting cheeks are
     mine,
A garden with fresh flowers all the winter;
Those lips invite to print my soul upon them,

23

Or lose it in thy breath, which I'll convey
Down to my heart, and wish no other spirit,
As loth to change it for my own again.
How in thy bosom will I dwell', Emeria,
And tell the azure winding of thy veins
That flow, yet climb those soft and ivory hills,
Whose smooth descent leads to a bliss that may
Be known, but puzzles art and tongue to speak it!
I prithee do not use this froward motion ;
I must, and will be thine.
   Em. Be your own, sir,
And do not thus afflict my innocence.
Had you the power of all the world, and man,
You could not force my will, which you have
      frighted
More from you, than my duty, although powerful,
Can call again.   You are not modest, sir,
Indeed I fear you are not.   I must leave you ;
Better desires attend your grace and me!   [*Exit.*
   Cor. This will not gain her; her heart's fix'd upon
My brother ; all my hope is in Archimagus.
She is a frozen thing, yet she may melt.
If their disdain should make a man despair,
Nature mistook in making woman fair.   [*Exit.*

SCENE II.

The Temple ; Ferochus *and* Endarius, *representing two Idols ; before them an altar, at which
stand* Archimagus *and* Magicians ; Rodamant
*is busied in arranging lights, and preparing
incense.*

   Rod. These be new deities, made since yesterday.
We shift our gods as fast as some shift trenchers.—
Pray, sir, what do you call their names? they are

But half gods, demi-gods, as they say ; there's nothing
Beneath the navel.
   Arch. This with the thunderbolt is Jupiter.
   Rod. Jupiter ! 'tis time he were cut off by the middle ;
He has been a notable thunderer in his days.
   1 *Mag.* This is Mars.
   Rod. Mars, from the middle upward. Was it by my lady Venus' direction that he is dismembered too? He that overcame all in a full career, looks now like a demi-lance.
   Arch. Are they not lively form'd ? But, sirrah, away !
Tell the young ladies the king is upon entrance.
                         [Exit Rod.

Enter, at one side, King, Queen, *and* CONALLUS; *at the other,* ETHNE, *and* FEDELLA, *followed by* RODAMANT ; *they all kneel, and the king places his crown upon the altar.*

   Arch. To Jove and Mars the king doth pay
His duty, and thus humbly lay
Upon [their] altar his bright crown,
Which is not his, if they but frown.—
In token you are pleas'd, let some
Celestial flame make pure this room.
            [A flame rises from behind the altar.
The gods are pleas'd, great king; and we
Return thy golden wreath to thee,
            [Replaces the crown on the king's head.
More sacred by our holy fume ;
None to the altar yet presume.
Now shoot your voices up to Jove,
To Mars, and all the powers above.

Song, at the altar.

Come away, oh, come away,
And trembling, trembling pay
Your pious vows to Mars and Jove.
 While we do sing,

Gums of precious odours bring,
And light them with your love ;
As your holy fires do rise,
[In cloudless glory to the skies,]
 Make Jove to wonder
 What new flame
 Thither came
To wait upon his thunder.
[After the song, the Queen, and her daugh-
 ters, offer garlands, which are placed
 upon the heads of the idols. The idol re-
 presenting Jupiter moves.

King. Archimagus! Conallus! see, my children,
The statue moves!
 Arch. Approach it not too near.
 Eth. It is prodigious!
 Arch. With devotion
Expect what follows, and keep reverend distance.
 [*King.*] I am all wonder.
 [*A voice speaks from the statue of Jupiter.*]
 King Leogarius,
Jove doth accept thy vows and pious offerings,
And will shower blessings on thee, and this kingdom,
If thou preserve this holy flame burns in thee ;
But, take heed thou decline not thy obedience,
Which thou shalt best declare by thy just anger
Against that Christian straggler Patrick, whose
Blood must be sacrificed to us, or you
Must fall in your remiss and cold religion.
When you are merciful to our despisers,
You pull our wrath upon you, and this island.
 VOL. IV. **D d**

My duty is perform'd, and I return
To my first stone, a cold and silent statue.
   Arch. What cannot all commanding Jove! 'tis
      now
That artificial tongueless thing it was.
How are you bound to honour Jupiter,
That, with this strange and public testimony,
Accepts your zeal! Pursue what you intended,
And meet this enemy to the gods, that now
Expects your entertainment.
   King. I obey.—
Come, my queen, and daughters.
   Queen. I attend you, sir.
   Rod. Is not the queen a lovely creature, sir?
   1 *Mag.* Why, how now, Rodamant, what pas-
      sion's this?
   Rod. Oh that I durst unbutton my mind to her!
   Arch. Your princely daughters pray they may
      have leave
To offer, in their gratitude to the gods,
One other prayer, and they will follow, sir.
   King. They are my pious daughters.—Come,
      Conallus.
             [*Exeunt King, Queen, Conallus, &c.*
   Arch. They are gone; uncloud.
                    [*Fer. and End. descend.*
   Fer. Oh, my dear mistress!—
Is not the king mock'd rarely?
   Eth. My most loved Endarius!
   Arch. Have I not done't, my charge?
   Fed. Most quaintly.—Welcome
To thy Fedella.
   Rod. Hum! how's this? more 'scapes of Jupi-
ter? They have found their nether parts; the
gods are become fine mortal gentlemen. Here's
precious juggling! if I durst talk on't.
   Arch. Not a syllable, as you desire not to be
torn in pieces, sir.

Rod. Gods, quotha! I held a candle before the devil.

Arch. To the door, and watch.

Rod. So, I must keep the door too; here's like to be holy doings.

Fer. We owe Archimagus for more than life,
For your loves, without which, life is a curse. [*Music.*

Arch. The music prompts you to a dance.

End. I' the temple!

Arch. 'Tis most secure; none dare betray you here.
　　　　　　　　　　　　　　　　　　　[*They dance.*

Eth. We must away.

Fer. My life is going from me.

Fed. Farewell.

Arch. The king expects. Now kiss, and part.

Eth. When next we meet, pray give me back
　　　　my heart.

Rod. I am an esquire,[1] by my office. [*Exeunt.*

ACT III.　SCENE I.

Before the Palace.

Enter RODAMANT.

Rod. Oh, my royal love!—Why should not I love the queen? I have known as simple a fellow as I hath been in love with her horse, nay, they have been bedfellows in the same litter; and in that humour he would have been leap'd, if the beast could have been provok'd to incontinency. But what if the king should know on't, and very lovingly circumcise me for it? or hang me up a gra-

---

[1] *I am an* esquire, &c.] This, with the other expressions of this facetious personage, such as "keeping the door," &c. all allude to the same honourable employment, that of procuring.

D d 2

cious spectacle, with my tongue out, a perch for sparrows? Why, I should become the gallows, o' my conscience. Oh, I would stretch in so gentle a posture, that the spectators all should edify, and hang by my example.—

Enter Bard.

The king's merry bard; if he have overheard, he'll save the hangman a labour, and rhyme me to death.

Bard. Rodamant, my half man, half goblin, all fool, how is't? When didst thou see the devil?

Rod. Alas, I never had the happiness.

Bard. Why, then thou art not acquainted with thy best friend. [*Sings.*

Have you never seen in the air,
One ride with a burning spear,
Upon an old witch with a pad,
For the devil a sore breech had,
　　With lightning and thunder,
　　And many more wonder,
　　His eyes indeed—la, sir!—
　　As wide as a saucer?
Oh, this would have made my boy mad.

Rod. An honest, merry trout.

Bard. Thou say'st right, gudgeon, gape, and I'll throw in a bushel. Why does thy nose hang over thy mouth, as it would peep in, to tell how many teeth thou hast?

Rod. Excellent bard! oh, brave bard! Ha, bard!

Bard. Excellent fool! oh, fine fool! Ha, fool!

Rod. Prithee with what news, and whither is thy head travelling?

Bard. My head and my feet go one way, and both now at their journey's end. The news is,

that one Patrick, a stranger, is invited to court:
this way he must come; and I, like one of the
king's wanton whelps, have broke loose from the
kennel, and come thus afore to bark, and bid
him welcome; the king and queen will meet him.

Rod. Has the king invited him?

Bard. What else, man? [*Sings.*

Oh, the queen and the king, and the royal offspring,
 With the lords and ladies so gay,
I tell you not a trick, to meet the man Pa-trick,
 Are all now trooping this way.
This man, report sings, does many strange things :
 Our priests, and our bards must give place ;
He cares not a straw for our sword or club-law.
 Oh, I long to behold his gay face.

Rod. Prithee, a word; thou didst name the
queen; does she come too?

Bard. By any means.

Rod. Well, 'tis a good soul.

Bard. Who?

Rod. The queen.

Bard. The queen is't? Dost make but a soul
of her? Treason! I have heard some foolish philo-
sophers affirm that women have no souls; 'twere
well for some they had no bodies; but to make no
body of the queen is treason, if it be not felony.

Rod. Oh, my royal love!

Bard. Love! art thou in love, Rodamant?
nay, then, thou may'st talk treason, or any thing.
Folly and madness are lash free, and may ride
cheek by jowl with a judge. But dost thou know
what love is, thou! one of Cupid's overgrown mon-
keys? Come, crack me this nut of love, and take
the maggot for thy labour.

Rod. Prithee, do thou say what 'tis.

Bard. No, I will sing a piece of my mind, and
love to thee. [*Sings.*

Love is a bog, a deep bog, a wide bog ;
Love is a clog, a great clog, a close clog;
'Tis a wilderness to lose ourselves,
A halter 'tis to noose ourselves.
Then draw Dun out o' the mire,
And throw the clog into the fire.
Keep in the king's highway,
And, sober, you cannot stray.
If thou admire no female elf,
The halter may go hang itself.
Drink wine, and be merry, for love is a folly,
And dwells in the house of melancholy.

Rod. 'Tis such a merry baboon, and shoots quills like a porcupine. But who's this?

Enter, at one side, St. Patrick, *and his train ; at the other, the* King, Queen, *his Sons and Daughters,* Milcho, Archimagus, *and* Magicians.

Bard. 'Tis he ; I know him by instinct. [*Sings.*

Patrick, welcome to this isle !
See how every thing doth smile :
To thy staff and thy mitre,
And lawn that is whiter,
And every shaven crown, a welcome, welcome to town!
Look where the king and queen do greet thee,
His princely sons are come to meet thee.
And see where a pair is of very fine fairies,
Prepar'd too,
That thou may'st report thy welcome to court ;
And the bard too.

And so pray, father, give me your blessing.

---

* *Then draw* Dun *out of the mire,*
    And throw the clog into the fire.]   For an explanation of this, see Jonson's works, vol. vii. p. 282.

St. P. I thank thee, courteous bard ; thy heart is
    honest.—
But to the king my duty.
    King. Welcome, Patrick,
For so thou call'st thyself ; we have thrown off
Our anger ; and with calm and melting eyes
Look on thee.   Thou hast piety to forgive
Our former threats and language ; and to satisfy
For our denial of some humble cottages,
Against the hospitable laws of nature,
We give thee now our palace, use it freely ;
Myself, our queen, and children, will be all
Thy guests, and owe our dwellings to thy favour.
There are some things of venerable mark
Upon thy brow ; thou art some holy man,
Design'd by Providence to make us happy :
Again most welcome to us.
    Queen. His aspéct
Doth promise goodness.—Welcome.
    Cor. To us all.
    St. P. If this be hearty, heaven will not permit
Your charities unrewarded.
    Cor. I am weary
Of these dull complements, Archimagus.
    Arch. I am prepar'd ; I know your blood's a
    longing
To change embraces with Emeria.
Receive this [gift], which, worn upon your arm,
Is so by power of magic fortified,
You shall go where you please invisible,
Until you take it off.   Go to your mistress.
                            [*Gives him a bracelet.*
    Cor. Softly, my dear Archimagus ; the rest
Speak in a whisper ; I shall be jealous of
The intelligencing air.
    King. You may be confident
Our favour spreads to all.   But where is Dichu,
Your convert ? we'll receive him to our grace too.

St. P. He durst not, sir, approach your royal
    presence ;
And grief for the sad fate of his two sons
Hath made him weary of society:
Not far off, in a wood, he means to wear out
His life in prayer and penance.
    Arch. How do you taste it?
    Cor. 'Tis rare, and must succeed to my ambition.
    Arch. Lose no time then.
    Cor. I fly.   Command me ever.   [*Exit Cor.*
    King. I am not well o' the sudden.
    Queen. How! what is't
That doth offend the king?
    King. An evil conscience.—
Alas, my children!
    Con. Father!
    Arch. Sir!
    Eth. Pray speak to us!
    King. How shall I
Win credit with this good man, that I have
Repented for the blood of Dichu's sons?
    St. P. If you dissemble not with heaven, I can
Be easily gain'd, sir, to believe, and pray for you.
    King. Some wine; it is the greatest ceremony
Of love with us, the seal of reconcilement.
Let some one bring us wine ; I will not move
Until I drink to this blest man.
    Arch. Away!   [*Exit Rod.*
    King. This place shall be remembered to pos-
    terity,
Where Leogarius first shew'd himself friend
To holy Patrick: 'tis religious thirst,
That will not let me expect till morn return.
There is a stream of peace within my heart.
    Arch. 'Tis rarely counterfeited.   [*Aside.*
    Con. He is my father,
I should else tell him 'tis not like a king,
Thus to conspire a poor man's death. What thinks

Our royal mother? Is it just to take
By stratagem this innocent man's life?
    Queen. What means my son?
    Con. Shall I betray the plot
Yet, and preserve him?—See, the wine.

        Re-enter RODAMANT, *with wine.*

    Arch. The wine
Attends you, sir.
    King. 'Tis well; fill us a cheerful cup.—Here,
        Patrick,
We drink thy welcome to the Irish coasts.
    Eth. What does my father mean to do with this
Dull thing? he'll never make a courtier.
    Fed. His very looks have turn'd my blood
        already.
    Arch. I'll spice his cup.
    King. Do't strongly.
    Queen. There's
Something within prompts me to pity this
Stranger.   [*Aside.*
    Con. Do you love wine, sir?
    St. P. If I did not,
I should presume, against my nature, once
To please the king, that hath thus honour'd us.
    Con. Do not; I say do not.   [*Aside to St. P.*
    Arch. Please you, sir?   [*Gives St. P. the cup.*
    King. Come, to our queen.
    Rod. My royal love! would I had the grace to
drink to her, or kiss the cup.
    St. P. My duty.   [*Drinks.*
    Arch. Now observe, sir, the change; he has it
        home.
    Rod. I cannot live, my heart will not hold out.
    King. Forbear, as you affect your life.
    Queen. How's this?
Now I suspect Conallus.   .   [*Aside.*

St. P. I have one boon to ask your majesty,
Since you look on us with this gracious smile,
That you would give my poor companions **leave**
To build a little chapel in this place,
(It shall be the first monument of your love,)
To use our own religion.   The ground offers
Plenty of stone, the cost and pain be our's.
   King. Not yet !   [*Aside.*
   St P. 'Twill bind us ever to pray for you.
   King. If it were violent as thou say'st, it **had**
By this time gnawn to his bowels.   [*To Arch.*
   St. P. Sir, you mind not
The humble suit I make.
   Arch. Not yet!
   St. P. Great sir.
   King. It does not alter him ; he rather **looks**
With fresher blood upon him.
   Arch. 'Tis my wonder ;
I did not trust another to prepare
His cup.
   King. Come, 'tis not poison ; we are abus'd.
   Arch. Upon my life.
   St. P. The king is troubled.
   King. Prepare another.
   Arch. It shall be done.
   King. Come hither, sirrah ; you brought **this**
      wine.
   Rod. I did, sir.
   King. And you shall taste it.
   Rod. Would I were but worthy !
   King. I will have it so.   Come, drink our health.
   Rod. May I remember your good queen's ?
   Arch. An he had the constitution of an elephant,
'Twould pay him.
   Queen. How cheer you, sir?
   St. P. Well, madam ; but I observe
Distractions in the king.
   King. Nay, drink it off.

Rod. An'twere as deep as the root of Penmenmaur,
My royal love should have it.   [*Drinks.*

King. Now we shall try the ingredients ;
It stirr'd not him.   Has he done it?

Rod. So.

Arch. Yes, and the change begins to shew
    already.

Rod. Hoy, ho !—What's that ?

Bard. Where ?

Rod. Here, hereabouts.   Was the wine burnt?
Oh, there's wildfire in the wine !

Arch. It works on him.

Rod. There's squibs and crackers in my stomach ; am not I poison'd?

Bard. Poison'd ! we shall want a fool then.

Rod. Away! I'll never drink again.

Bard. Not often, an thou be'st poison'd.

Rod. It increases ; my royal love has poison'd
me ; her health has blown my bowels up.   Oh, a
cooler ; would I were a while in the frozen sea !
charity is not cold enough to relieve me : the devil
is making fireworks in my belly.   Ha! the queen !
let me but speak to the queen.—Oh, madam, little
do you think that I have poison'd myself—oh,—for
your sweet sake.   But, howsoever. — Oh, think
upon me when I am dead.   I bequeath my heart.
—Oh, there 'tis already.   My royal love, farewell.
                    [*Falls senseless.*

Arch. What think you now? it hath despatch'd
    him raving.

St. P. Madam, you shew a pious heart.
I find my death was meant : but 'tis heaven's
    goodness
I should not fall by poison : do not lose
Your charity.

Bard. He's dead.

St. P. Pray let me see the fellow.

King. It affrights me;
This was some treason meant to us, and thee,
Good man. How[ever] I am innocent.
    St. P. How soon death would devour him !
    Arch. Past your cure.
    St. P. That Power we serve can call back life;
        and, see,
He has a little motion.
    Bard. He breathes too ; nay, then, he may live
to have t' other cup.—Madam, this Patrick is a
rare physician ; if he stay with us, he'll make us
all immortal.
    King. Alive again ? Oh, let me honour thee.
    Queen. We cannot, sir, enough. Receive me,
        Patrick,
A weak disciple to thee ; my soul bids me
Embrace thy faith : make me a Christian.
    King. How! Didst thou hear, Archimagus!
        let some
Convey our queen hence, her weak conscience
        melts ;
She'll be a Christian, she says : I hate her,
And do confine her to the house of Milcho,
Our zealous provost.
    Mil. 'Tis the king's pleasure, madam,
I should attend you hence.
    Queen. Where the king pleases.
    St. P. In any prison, madam, I dare visit you.
Be comforted, they do but fight with heaven.
    Con. I'll wait upon my mother.
               [*Exeunt Mil. Queen, and Con.*
    King. Look to my daughters,
Lest this change work on them.
    Arch. They are my charge.
    King. Be not dejected, Patrick ; we do mean
All good to thee. Set forward. Have a care
Of that poor fellow.

St. P. I'll attend you, sir ;
And trust to Providence we shall be safe.

> [*Exeunt all but Bard and Rod.*

Bard. How is't now, Rodamant? Dost thou
remember thou wert dead? thou wert poison'd.

Rod. There is a kind of grumbling in my guts
still.

Bard. [sings.]—*Come, we will drink a cup, boy,*
> *but of better brewing,*
And we will drink it up, joy, without any fear of s—
Wine is unjust that is taken on trust ; if it tarry
> *with us it fats.*
A cup, boy, drink up, joy, and let 'em go poison rats.

> [*Exeunt.*

SCENE II.

An Apartment in the Palace.

Enter EMERIA *with a key.*

Em. What is it that doth sit so heavy on me?
Since Corybreus talk'd with me I find
A dulness in my brain, and my eyes look
As through a mist, which hangs upon my lids,
And weighs them down. He frighted me to hear
> him.
He has a rugged and revengeful nature ;
Not the sweet temper that his brother [owns.]
My dear Conallus.—Mine? alas! did I
Say mine? indeed he is master of my heart,
But something makes me fear I shall not be
So happy as I wish in his possession :
Yet we have vows on both sides, holy ones,
And marriage promis'd. But I am too loud.
Yet not, my lodgings are remote, and privat'st

38

Of all the court ; and I have dismiss'd the servants ;
None near to reach my voice ; then, till this give
Access, [*locks the door.*] I need not fear the silent
    chambers.
More clouds do gather 'bout my eyes ; 'tis strange,
I am not used to be inclin'd to sleep
While the day shines ; then take what nature offers,
Emeria, and comply ; it may discharge
Thy waking melancholy. So ;   [*Lies down.*
I feel it gently slide upon my senses.   [*Sleeps.*

Enter Spirits before CORYBREUS, *habited gloriously,
and representing the god Ceanerachius. The
Spirits disappear.*

Cor. So, so! this amulet, I find, secures me
From all observers, and I now am in
Her chamber, by a feat my spirits did me.—
Ha! she sleeps too ; what a fine bawd the devil is!
What opportunities he can frame to bring
These things to pass! I were best lose no time.—
Madam! madam! fair Emeria!
    Em. Ha!
Who is that? was it a voice that call'd me,
Or do I dream? Here's no body ; this key
Made all without fast ; yet I'll see.
                [*Rises, and goes to the door.*
    Cor. I had
Forgot ; she'll never see me, if I do not
Take off my charm ; perhaps I may again
Be visible, if I have not lost myself.
    Em. The doors are fast. [*Music.*] — Ha! bless
    me, you powers!
This music is not frequent in my chambers ;
'Tis here,—I know not where ; I can see nothing.
    Cor. Emeria!

Em. Who is't that calls Emeria?—Goodness aid
    me!   [*Takes off the bracelet.*
  Cor. Put off thy fright, Emeria; yet I blame not
Thy feeble sense, to tremble at my presence;
Not us'd to mortal eyes, and unprepar'd.
But gather strength, and call thy blood again,
Whose seat a paleness doth usurp : I am
Thy friend.
  - *Em.* But no acquaintance sure ; what are you?
  Cor. Not what I seem ; I have assum'd this
    form,
To tell thee what a happiness is now
Coming from heaven upon thee.
  Em. Upon me?
  Cor. And when the sweet Emeria is collected,
She will lose her life again in joy and wonder.
  Em. My strength returns ; this is a gentle lan-
    guage ;
And, spirit, if thou be'st one, speak thy will.
  Cor. Then know, Emeria, I am no mortal,
But Ceanerachius, chief of all the gods,
That now appear.
  Em. I know not what to answer,
But with my humble knee.   [*Kneels.*
  Cor. Thy pure devotion,
Richer than clouds of incense, myrrh, and cassia,
And all the gums, whose piles make sweet our
    altar,
Hath been delightful to the gods, and me ;
And I have left the palace of the blest,
Where many glorious virgins wait, and want
    thee,
A fellow singer in their heavenly quire,
To visit in this form the fair Emeria,
And thank thee for thy pious sacrifices.
Rise then, and be confirm'd ; we mean to honour
Thy person and thy virtues.
  Em. Can this roof

Be so much blest? and can so great a deity
Consider my imperfect duty thus?
    Cor. To assure thy thoughts, ask, fairest virgin,
        what
Thou most desirest, and it shall, firmer than
The Destinies, be made thine own.   Hast thou
A wish to this world's glory, to be greater?
Would'st thou enlarge thy knowledge, or thy plea-
        sure?
Dost thou affect to have thy life extended
Double the course of nature? or thy beauty
Above the malice of disease, or time
To wither?   Would'st thou see thy book of fate,
And read the various lines that fall into
Thy life, as to their centre? Speak, and be
Possess'd; if thou refuse what here is named,
Thy wish will come too late, Emeria.
    Em. None of all these. Let me be still accepted
An humble servant to the gods.
    Cor. Then I
Will find some other way to thy reward:
First, we release that duty of thy knee;
Reach thy fair hand.
    Em. I dare not.
    Cor. Do not tremble,   *[Raises her.*
It shall but meet another like thine own,
For I had care not to affright my virgin.
What dost thou see in me, that, to thy sense,
Appears not man? Divinity is too bright
For thy weak eye, and therefore I have clad,
In this no-threat'ning shape, all that is divine,
That I, with safety of thy sense, Emeria,
Might visit thee.   Come, I will see thee often,
If thou be wise to understand how much
It is my will to honour thee; and I
Will thus descend, and leave my beams behind,
Whose brightness were enough to burn thee,
To converse with thee in a loving way

Of smiling thus, and thus embracing thee—
Of mixing palms ; nay, I will kiss thee too.
   Em. Do our gods practise this ?
   Cor. Not but with those
They mean especial grace to ; such as they
Know must hereafter shine above with them,
Though merely mortals, are ador'd ;   *   *
*   *   *   *   *   *   *
*   *   *   *   *   and seldom '
Visit the world, hid thus in flesh and blood,
Which we at pleasure can assume, and have
Desires like you, and have our passions too,
Can love, ay, and enjoy where we will place
The happiness, else we had [been] less than men.
   Em. I thought the powers above had been all
        honest.
   Cor. 'Tis in them chastity ; nor is it sin
In those we love, to meet with active flames,
And be glad mothers to immortal issues.
How oft hath Jove, who justly is adored,
Left heaven, to practise love with such a fair one !
The Sun, for one embrace of Daphne, would
Have pawn'd his beams ; not one but hath some-
        times
Descended, to make fruitful weak mortality.
Oh, if thou could'st but reach, Emeria,
With thy imagination, what delight,
What flowing ecstasies of joy we bring
Your sex, made nice and cold by winter's laws
Of man, that freeze the blood, thou would'st be fond

---

    * *Though merely mortals, are adored ;*   *   *   *
      *   *   *   *   *   *
      *   *   *   *and seldom,* &c.] This speech is
given in the old copy as prose, and most ridiculously pointed :
these however are accidents in Shirley too common to be noticed ; but it appears that the careless printer has also suffered
some of the copy to escape his eye. It is in vain to guess at
what we have lost ; but Corybreus, after adverting to deified
mortals, seems to revert to the privileges of the gods themselves.
   VOL. IV.   E e

Of my embraces, and petition me
To bless thee with a rape! yet I woo thy
Consent.

Em. Away! thou art no god sure, but
Some vicious impostor. Can a deity
Breathe so much impious language, and reward
Virtue with shame?

Cor. Take heed, and do not ruin[2]
Thyself by rash and froward opposition;
Know, I can make thee nothing at a breath.

Em. Better be so, than made so foul a being.

Cor. Nay, then, what should have been with thy
     consent
A blessing, shall now only serve my pleasure,
And I will take the forfeit of thy coldness.

Em. Oh, help! some man! I dare not call upon
The gods, for they are wicked grown. Oh, help!

Cor. I shall need none, thou thing of disobe-
     dience;
Thou art now within my power of love, or fury:
Yield, or I'll force thee into postures shall
Make pleasure weep, and hurl thee into wantonness.
     [*Bears her in, while Spirits are seen rejoicing
          in a dance.*

ACT IV. SCENE I.

A Room in Milcho's *House.*

Enter MILCHO *and* Servant.

Mil. Who's with the queen, my prisoner?
Serv. The prince
Conallus came to visit her.
Mil. So! bid
My daughter Emeria come hither.—She is
          [*Exit Serv.*

[2] For *ruin*, the old copy reads *vaine.*

43

Come very melancholy from the court,
Under pretence to wait upon the queen here.—

Enter EMERIA.

Still sad! come, I must have your face look otherwise,
Dress it in smiles : I hope you put not on
This sorrow for the queen ; she is a traitor
To the king, and to the gods.
 Em. A traitor, sir!
Oh, do not say so ; 'tis, I hear, for nothing
But looking on the stranger Patrick with
Some pity.
 Mil. It will not run
Out of my thought, but this is the same Patrick
That was my slave once ; he was a Briton too ;
I know not how, he found some treasure then
To buy his liberty : were he again
My slave, no gold should buy him from my swine,
Whose once companion he was.—Emeria,
Do you hear? Conallus, the young prince, is come
To see his mother ; use him gently, girl.
Come, I have heard he does affect thee, ha?
He may be king.
 Em. His brother, Corybreus,
Is nearer to that title, and he says
He loves me.
 Mil. Does he so? then love him best.
 Em. Imagine I had promis'd, sir, my heart
To his younger brother.
 Mil. Break a thousand promises,
And hazard breaking of thy heart too, wench,
To be but one degree nearer a queen.
It does exalt my heart ; spread all thy charms
Of wit and language when he courts thee, girl ;
Smile, kiss, or any thing that may endear
Him, and so great a fortune : I must leave thee,
But will not be long absent.
     E e 2

Re-enter Servant.

Serv. Sir, the bard
Does press to see the queen.
    Mil. He must not see her,
His insolence I'll punish: yet admit him [*Exit Serv.*
Hither; his pleasant nature may raise mirth
In my sad daughter.—

Enter Bard.

Welcome, merry bard.
    Bard. I care not whether I be or no : the queen
I come to see.
    Mil. She's private with the prince.—
Come hither. Dost thou see that piece of sullenness,
That phlegmatic foolish thing?
    Bard. And like the father.
    Mil. Make her merry, and I'll give thee
Gold, joy, to purchase a new harp ; here's some
In earnest ; thou hast wanton pretty songs,
To stir the merry thoughts of maids. I'm gone,
To give thee opportunity ; my presence
May spoil the working of thy mirth ; that done,
Shalt speak with the queen too.   [*Exit.*
    Bard. Fare you well, sir,
And take a knave along with you. Here's a rose
Sprung out of a thistle now !—You are sad, madam.
    Em. I have no cause of mirth, bard.
    Bard. What do you think
Of me?
    Em. Think of thee, bard ! I think
Thou'rt honest, and canst shew a pleasant face
Sometimes, without an over joy within ;
But 'tis thy office.
    Bard. I know why you are
So melancholy.
    Em. Prithee why, dost think, bard?
    Bard. You want a man.
    Em. Why, thou art one.

Bard. That's more than you know.   [*Sings.*

> '*Tis long of men that maids are sad,*
>   *Come then, and sweetly kiss them ;*
> *Their lips invite, you will be mad*
>   *To come too late, and miss them.*
> *In their cheeks are full-blown roses,*
>   *To make garlands, to make posies.*
>   *He that desires to be a father,*
> *Let him make haste before they fall, and gather ;*
>   *You stay too long, and do them wrong :*
> *If men would virgins strive to please,*
> *No maid this year should die o' the green*
>   *disease.*

What, are you merry yet ?
  Em. I am so far
From being rais'd to mirth, that I incline
To anger.
  Bard. Come, I'll fit you with a song,
A lamentable ballad, of one lost
Her maidenhead; and would needs have it cried,
With all the marks, in hope to have it again.
  Em. You were not sent to abuse me ?
  Bard. A dainty air too ; I'll but tune my instru-
    ment.
  Em. No more, or I'll complain.—Sure he knows
    nothing
Of my dishonour. How mine own thoughts fright me !
  Bard. Now you shall hear the ditty.
  Em. Hence, foolish bard !   [*He sings.*

> *A poor wench was sighing, and weeping amain,*
> *And fain would she have her virginity again,*
> *Lost she knew not how ; in her sleep, as she said,*
> *She went to bed pure, but she risse not a maid.*
>   *She made fast the door,*
>   *She was certain, before*
>   *She laid herself down in the bed ;*
> *But when she awaked, the truth is, stark-naked,*
>   *Oh, she miss'd her maidenhead.*

Enter Conallus.

Ha! the young prince! I'll tarry no longer with
    you.—
Now to the queen.   [*Exit.*
   Con. Emeria, prithee do not hide thy face
From me ; 'tis more than common sorrow makes
Thee look thus.   If the queen's misfortunes have
Darken'd thy face, I suffer too in that ;
If for thyself thou weep'st, my almost ebbing
Grief thou wilt enforce back, and [thus] beget
New seas, in which, made high by one strong sigh
Of thine, I meet a watry sepulchre.
My mother's fate commands my grief, but thine
A greater suffering, since our hearts are one,
And there wants nothing but a ceremony
To justify it to the world.
   Em. Call back
Your promises, my lord, they were ill placed
On me, for I have nothing to deserve them.
   Con. If thou be'st constant to thyself, and art
Emeria still—
   Em. That word hath wounded me.
   Con. Why, art not thou thyself?
   Em. I have the shape still,
But not the inward part.
   Con. Am I so miserable,
To have my faith suspected, for I dare not
Think thou canst sin by any change.   What act
Have I done, my Emeria ? or who hath
Poison'd thy pure soul with suggestion
Of my revolt? apostasy, I'll call it,
For, next our gods, thou art my happiness.
   Em. Now, my dear lord, and let me add thus
    much
In my own part, I never loved you better ;
Never with more religious thoughts and honour

Look'd on you ; my heart never made a vow
So blessed in my hopes, as that I gave you,
And I suspect not your's.
    Con. What then can make thee,
My Emeria, less, or me ? Thou dost affright—
    Em. Yes, I am less, and have that taken from me
Hath almost left me nothing ; or, if any,
So much unworthy you, that you would curse me,
Should I betray you to receive Emeria.
    Con. Do not destroy me so ; be plain.
    Em. Then thus——
But if I drop a tear or two, pray pardon me :
Did not the story touch myself, I should
Weep for it in another ; you did promise
To marry me, my lord.
    Con. I did, and will.
    Em. Alas, I have lost—
    Con. What?
    Em. The portion that
I promis'd to bring with me.
    Con. Do I value
Thy wealth?
    Em. Oh, but the treasure
I lost, you will expect, and scorn me ever,
Because you have it not ; yet heaven is witness
'Tis not my fault, a thief did force it from me.
Oh, my dear lord !
    Con. I know not what to fear ;
Speak plainer yet.
    Em. You'll say I am too loud,
When I but whisper, sir, I am—no virgin.
    Con. Ha!
    Em. I knew 'twould fright you ; but, by all those
        tears,
The poor lamb, made a prey to the fierce wolf,
Had not more innocence, or less consent
To be devoured, than I to lose mine honour.
    Con. Why, wert thou ravish'd?

Em. You have named it, sir.

Con. The villain! name the villain, sweet
    Emeria,
That I may send his leprous soul to hell for't;
And when he hath confess'd the monstrous sin,
I'll think thee still a virgin, and thou art so:
Confirm thy piety by naming him.

Em. It will enlarge but your vexation, sir,
That he's above your anger and revenge;
For he did call himself a god that did it.

Con. The devil he was. Oh, do not rack, Emeria,
The heart that honours thee; mock me not, I pri-
    thee,
With calling him a god; it was a fury,
The master fiend of darkness, and as hot
As hell could make him, that would ravish thee.

Em. If you do think I ever loved you, sir,
Or have a soul after my body's rape,
He nam'd himself a god, great Ceanerachius,
To whom I owe my shame and transformation.

Con. Oh, I am lost in misery and amazement.
                      [*Exit.*

Em. So! I did see before it would afflict him:
But having given these reasons to Conallus,
For our divorce, I have provided how
To finish all disgraces, by my death.
                [*Shews a poniard.*
Come, cure of my dishonour, and with blood

Enter ARCHIMAGUS.

Wash off my stain.—Ha! Archimagus!

Arch. Madam.

Em. What news with our great priest?

Arch. I come to tell you, heavenly Ceanerachius,
Of whom I had this day a happy vision,
Is pleas'd again to visit you, and commanded
I should prepare you.

Em. I begin to find
Some magical imposture.   Does he know it?
                                                    [*Aside.*
  Arch. I leave to say how much you are his
    favourite ;
Be wise, and humble for so great a blessing.
  Em. This does encrease my fears I've been
    betray'd ;
I'll live a little longer then. [*aside.*]—Great priest,
My words are poor, to make acknowledgment
For so divine a favour : but I shall
Humbly expect, and hold myself again
Blest in his presence.

    Enter CORYBREUS, *habited as before.*

  Arch. He's here, Emeria ;
Never was virgin so much honoured.   [*Exit.*
  Cor. How is it with my sweet Emeria?
  Em. That question would become an ignorant
    mortal,
Whose sense would be inform'd ; not Ceanera-
    chius,
Whose eye at once can see the soul of all things.
  Cor. I do not ask, to make
Thee think I doubt, but to maintain that form,
Which men, familiar to such fair ones, use
When they converse ; for I would have my language
Soft as a lover's.
  Em. You are still gracious.
  Cor. This temper is becoming, and thou dost
Now appear worthy of our loves and presence.
I knew, when thy wise soul examin'd what
It was to be the darling to a god,
Thou would'st compose thy gestures, and resign
Thyself to our great will ; which we accept,
And pardon thy first frailty : 'tis in us,

50

Emeria, to translate thee hence to heaven,
Without thy body's separation,
I' the twinkling of an eye ; but thou shalt live,
Here to convince erring mortality,
That gods do visit such religious votaries
In human form, and thus salute them.

       [*Offers to kiss her*.

 Em. And thus be answer'd, with a resolute heart.

        [*Stabs him.*

 Cor. Oh, thou hast murdered me! Strumpet,
  hold!

 Em. Sure, if you be a god, you are above
These wounds ; if man, thou hast deserv'd to bleed
For thy impiety.

 Cor. My blood is punish'd.
A curse upon thy hand! I am no god ;
I am the prince: see, Corybreus.

 Em. Ha!
The prince! were you my ravisher, my lord ?
I have done a justice to the gods in this,
And my own honour. Thou lost thing to good-
  ness!
It was a glorious wound, and I am proud
To be the gods' revenger.

 Cor. Help! oh, I am lost!   [*Dies.*

 Em. Call on the furies, they did help thy sin,
And will transport thy soul on their black wings
To hell, prince ; and the gods can do no less
Than, in reward, to draw thy purple stream up,
Shed in their cause, and place it a portent
In heaven, to affright such foul lascivious princes.
I will live now ; this story shall not fall so ;
And yet I must not stay here. Now, Conallus,
I have done some revenge for thee in this ;
Yet all this will not help me to my own again ;
My honour of a virgin never will
Return : I live, and move ; but wanting thee,
At best I'm but a walking misery.   [*Exit.*

Enter RODAMANT, *reading a paper.*

Rod. *My royal love, my lady, and fair misteres,*
  Such love as mine was never read in histories.
There's *love,* and *love ;* good.
  The poison to my heart was not so cruel,
  As that I cannot hang thee—
How's that? hang the queen?
  The poison to my heart was not so cruel,
  As that I cannot hang thee, my rich jewel,
  Within my heart.—
Oh, there's *hang,* and *jewel,* and *heart,* and *heart ;*
Good again.
            I am thy constant elf,
  And dare, for thy sweet sake, go hang myself.
  What, though I am no lord, yet I am loyal ;
There's a gingle upon the letter, to shew, if she
will give me but an inch, I'll take an ell ; *lord,*
and *loyal.*
  And though no prince, I am thy servant royal.
There's no figure in that ; yes, impossibility, *ser-
vant* and *royal.*
  Then grant him love for love, that doth present
      these,
  With Noverint universi per presentes.
There's to shew I am a linguist, with a rum in the
rhyme,[*] consisting of two several languages, beside
love and *love.*
  Thy jet and alabaster face—
Jet, because it draws the straw of my heart, and
alabaster, because there is some white in her face.
  Thy jet and alabaster face now calls
  My love and hunger up, to eat stone walls.
But so I may bite off her nose, if her face be ala-
baster ; but she is in prison ; there it holds, and I

---

[*] *With a rum in the rhyme.*] So the 4to. It is probably the
fragment of a word, of which the rest was lost at the press.
Conundrum might have stood in the copy.

may do her service, to break prison for her any
way. Well, here's enough at a time; if she like
this, I have an ambling muse, that shall be at her
service. But what stumbling block is cast in my
way? This is no place to sleep in, I take it, in a
story under a trundle-bed. I have seen these
clothes afore now; the tailor took measure for one
of our gods, that made them.—Do you hear, friend?
[turns up the body.]—Ha! 'tis the prince Corybreus; dead, kill'd, ha!—My lord!—He's speech-
less. What were I best to do? Instead of search-
ing the wound, I'll first search his pockets. What's
here? a bracelet, a pretty toy; [puts it up.]—I'll
give it the queen; but if I be found here alone, I
may be found necessary to his death. Ha! what
shall I do?   [Hides himself.

       Re-enter MILCHO and Servant.

    Mil. My daughter gone abroad without a servant?
    Serv. I offer'd my attendance.
    Mil. Ha! what's here,
One murder'd? 'tis the prince! slain in my house!
Confusion! Look about, search for the traitor;
I am undone for ever.
    Serv. The prince! I'll take my oath I saw him
        not enter.
Why thus disguised?
       [While they examine the body, Rod. steals out.
    Mil. I tremble to look on him;   .
Seek every where.
    Serv. I gave access to none
But Rodamant, and he is gone.
    Mil. What shall we do? remove the murder'd
        body,
And on thy life be silent; we are lost else.
Attend without, and give access to none,
Till I have thought some way through this affliction.
                                               [Exit Serv.

Did my stars owe me this? Oh, I could curse them,
And from my vexed heart exhale a vapour
Of execrations, that should blast the day,
And darken all the world. The prince murder'd
In my house, and the traitor not discover'd!

Re-enter Servant.

Serv. One, sir, with a letter.
Mil. Let him carry it back.
Where's the young prince Conallus?
Serv. Gone long since, sir.
Mil. I'll lay the murder upon him; it will
Be thought ambition: or upon the queen.
Serv. Sir, one waits with a letter from the king.
Mil. The king? that name shoots horror through
    me now.
Who is the messenger?
Serv. A stranger both in habit and in person.

Enter St. PATRICK, *with a letter.*

This is he, sir.
Mil. Ha!
St. P. The king salutes you,
My lord; this paper speaks his royal pleasure.
                        [*Gives the letter.*
You have forgot me, sir; but I've been more
Familiar to your knowledge. Is there nothing
Within my face that doth resemble once
A slave you had?
Mil. Ha! is your name Patrick?
St. P. It is, my lord; I made my humble suit
To the king, that by his favour I might visit you;
And though I have not now that servile tie,
It will not shame me, to profess I owe

You duty still, and shall, to my best power,
Obey your just commands.
   Mil. He writ[es] to me,
That I should try my art, and by some stratagem
Discharge his life : I'll do it ; but all this will not
Quit the suspicion of the prince's death.
What if I lay the murder to his charge ?
I can swear any thing :—but if he come off,
My head must answer. No trick in my brain ?—
                             [*Aside.*
You're welcome ; the king writes you have desires
To see the queen ; you shall.—Entreat her presence.
                            [*Exit Serv.*

   St. P. The king has honour'd me.
   Mil. You have deserv'd it ;
And I do count it happiness to receive
Whom he hath graced ; but the remembrance
Of what you were, adds to the entertainment :
My old acquaintance, Patrick !
   St. P. You are noble.

     Re-enter Servant, with Queen *and* Bard.

   Mil. The queen ! Welcome again. —·Come
      hither, sirrah.   [*To Serv.*
   St. P. Madam, I joy to see you, and present
My humble duty. Heaven hath heard my prayers,
I hope ; and if you still preserve that goodness,
That did so late, and sweetly shine upon you,
I may not be unwelcome ; since there is
Something behind, which I am trusted with,
To make you happier.
   Queen. Holy Patrick, welcome.
   Mil. Obey in every circumstance.—My despair
                       [*Exit Serv.*
Shall have revenge wait on it.—This is, madam,
A good man ; he was once my slave—let not
That title take thy present freedom off.
My house, my fortunes, and my fate, I wish

May have one period with thee ; I shall
Attend you again.   I hope we all may live,
And die together yet.—My duty, madam.   [*Exit*
    Bard. I do not like their whispering ; there's
      some mischief,
He did so overact his courtesy.
I'll look about us.   [*Exit.*
    St. P. Do, honest bard. —Oh, madam, if you knew
The difference betwixt my faith and your
Religion, the grounds and progress of
What we profess ; the sweetness, certainty,
And full rewards of virtue, you would hazard,
Nay lose, the glory of ten thousand worlds
Like this, to be a Christian ; and be blest
To lay your life down, (but a moment, on
Which our eternity depends,) and through
Torture and seas of blood contend, to reach
That blessed vision at last, in which
Is all that can be happy, and perfection.
    Queen. I have a soul most willing to be taught.

Re-enter Bard *hastily.*

    Bard. Oh, madam ! fire ! help ! we are all lost ;
The house is round about on fire ! the doors
Are barr'd and lock'd, there is no going forth ;
We shall be burnt, and that will spoil my singing :
My voice hath been recover'd from a cold,
But fire will spoil it utterly.

Enter VICTOR.

    Vict. Have no dread, holy Patrick, all their
      malice
Shall never hurt thy person.   Heaven doth look
With scorn upon their treachery ; thou art
Reserv'd to make this nation glorious,
By their conversion to the christain faith,
Which shall, by blood of many martyrs, grow,

56

Till it be call'd the island of the saints.
  [*Flames are seen above, and Milcho casting
      various articles into them.*
Look up, and [say] what thou observest.*
  Mil. Patrick, thou art caught ; inevitable flames
Must now devour thee ; thou'rt my slave again,
There is no hope to 'scape.   How I do glory,
That by my policy thou shalt consume,
Though I be made a sacrifice with thee
To our great gods!—Ha ! ha! the queen.   Bard,
You will be excellent roast meat for the devil.
  St. P. Hear me.
  Mil. I choose to leap into these fires,
Rather than hear thee preach thy cursed faith.
You're sure to follow me ; the king will praise
My last act yet.   Thus I give up my breath,
And sacrifice you all for his son's death.
                [*Throws himself into the flames.*
  St. P. Oh, tyrant, cruel to thyself ! but we
Must follow our blest guide, and holy guardian.—
Lead on, good angel.—Fear not, virtuous queen ;
A black night may beget a smiling morn ;
At worst, to die 'tis easier than be born. [*Exeunt.*

SCENE II.

The Temple ; FEROCHUS *and* ENDARIUS *representing two Idols, as before. Recorders : then
enter* King, CONALLUS, ARCHIMAGUS, *Magicians.*
ETHNE, *and* FEDELLA. ARCHIMAGUS *offers a
sacrifice of human blood on the altar.*

Arch. Great Jove and Mars, appeased be
With blood, which we now offer thee,
Drain'd from a Christian's heart ; our first
Oblation of that sect accurs'd ;

---

  * *Look up, and* [*say*] *what thou observest.*]   After this the 4to.
reads : - - - - - - - - - " *Milcho*
        Throwing his treasures into the flames."
¬hich seems to be the stage direction, jumbled into the text.

And may we to the altar bring
Patrick, our second offering,
The father of this tribe, whose blood
Thus shed, will do this island good.—
    [A flame rises from behind the altar.
The gods allow what we present;
For see, the holy flame is sent!
To mighty Jove and Mars now bring
Your vocal sacrifice, and sing. ·

Song, at the altar.

Look down, great Jove, and god of war,
  A new sacrifice is laid
  On your altars, richer far
Than what in aromatic heaps we paid :
  No curled smoke we send,
  With perfumes, to befriend
  The drooping air ; the cloud
 We offer is exhaled from blood,
 More shining than your tapers are,
 And every drop is worth a star.
Were there no red in heaven, from the torn heart
Of Christians we that colour could impart ;
And with their blood supply those crimson streaks
That dress the sky, when the fair morning breaks.

Enter Rodamant, *and whispers the King, who falls*
    upon the ground.

 Con. Father !
 Arch. The king !
 King. Away ! let not my daughters stir from
  hence.
Is this reward, you gods, for my devotion ?
    [Rises, and exit with Conallus.
 · *Arch.* No more. I could not by my art foresee
This danger.
 vol. iv.   F f

Eth. Our father seem'd much troubled.

Arch. I must appear a stranger to all passages.
Be not disturb'd, my princely charge; use you
The free delights of life, while they are presented
In these your lovers.—Sirrah, make fast the door,
And wait aloof. I'll follow the sad king.

[*Exit.—Fer. and Endarius descend.*

Fed. No misery can happen, while I thus
Embrace Ferochus.

Eth. And I safe in the arms
Of my dear servant.

End. You make it heaven,
By gracing me.

Fer. But why have we so long
Delay'd our blest enjoyings, thus content
With words, the shadows of our happiness?

Rod. So, so! here's fine devotion in the temple!
But where's my bracelet? let me see.

[*Puts on the bracelet.*

Fer. Where's Rodamant?

Rod. Am I invisible again? Is this the trick
on't?

Fer. The door is safe. Come, my dear princely
mistress,
And with the crown of love reward your servant.

Fed. What's that?

Fer. Fruition of our joys.

Fed. Is not this
Delight enough, that we converse, and smile,
And kiss, Ferochus? [*Rod. kisses Fed.*]—Who's
that?

Fer. Where, madam?

Fed. I felt another lip.

Fer. Than mine? Here's none; try it again.—
Why should her constitution be so cold?
I would not lose more opportunities;
Love shoot a flame like mine into her bosom!

[*Aside.—Rod. kisses Ethne.*

Eth. Who's that, Endarius, that kiss'd me now?
End. None, since you blest my lip with a touch,
    madam.
My brother is at play with your fair sister.
    Eth. I felt a beard.
    End. A beard? that's strange.
    Rod. You shall feel some[thing] else too.
                [*He strikes End.*
    End. Why that unkind blow, madam?
    Eth. What means my servant?
    Rod. Now to my other gamester.
    Fer. Oh, I could dwell for ever in this bosom.
But is there nothing else for us to taste?—
        [*Rod. pulls Fer. by the nose.*
Hold!
    Fed. What's the matter?
    Fer. Something has almost torn away my nose.—
Endarius.
    End. What says my brother?
    Fer. Did you pull me by the nose?
    End. I moved not hence.—   [*Rod. kicks End.*
Did you kick me, brother?
    Fed. We have troubled fancies, sure; here's
    no body but ourselves;
The doors, you say, are safe.
    Fer. Will not that prompt you
To something else?
    Fed. I dare not understand you.—
        [*Rod. touches Ferochus' face with blood.*
What blood is that upon your face?
    Rod. You want
A beard, young gentleman.
        [*Rod. touches Endarius' chin with blood.*
    Fer. Mine? blood! I felt
Something, that like a fly glanced o' my cheek.—
Brother, [did] your nose bleed you that fine beard?
    End. You need not blush o' one side, brother;
    ha! ha!

F f 2

Eth. Is not this strange, sister? how came our
    servants
So bloody?   [*Rod. touches Fer. again with blood.*
    Fer. Again!
I prithee leave this fooling with my face,
I shall be angry.
    End. I touch'd you not.
    Rod. Another wipe for you.
                    [Touches End. again.
    Eth. Some spirit, sure : I cannot contain [my]
    laughter. —
What a raw head my servant has!
    Fed. Mine has the same complexion.
    Rod. Put me to keep the door another time! I
have kept them honest, and now I will be visible
again.
    [*Lies down, and takes off the bracelet.—Knock-
    ing within.*
    Fer. Rodamant!
    Rod. [*starting up.*]—Here! I was asleep, but
    this noise wak'd me.
Have you done with the ladies?
    [*Within.*]—Open the doors!

Enter Magician.

Mag. We are undone, my lords! the king is
    coming
In fury back again, with full resolve
To break these images.   His son is slain,
And burnt to ashes since, in Milcho's house ;
And he will be revenged upon the gods,
He says, that would not save his dearest son :
I fear he will turn Christian.   Archimagus
Is under guard, and brought along to see
This execution done.   No art can save you !
    Eth. We are lost too for ever, in our honours.
    King. [*within.*]—Break down the temple doors!

Mag. He's come already! we are all lost,
    madam!

Fer. Tear off these antique habits quickly; bro-
    ther,
Do you the same. More blood upon our faces.—
          [*They smear their faces with blood.*
Oh, my Fedella, something may preserve us
To meet again.—Endarius, so, so. Open.

Enter King, ARCHIMAGUS, *and* Guard; FEROCHUS
   and ENDARIUS *confidently meet the* King.

King. Ha! keep off! more horrors to affright me?
I must confess I did command your deaths
Unjustly, now my son is murder'd for it.

Fer. Oh, do not pull more wrath from heaven
    upon you.
Love innocence, the gods have thus revenged
In your son's tragedy. Draw not a greater
Upon yourself, and this fair island, by
Threat'ning the temples, and the gods themselves.
Look on them still with humble reverence,
Or greater punishments remain for you
To suffer, and our ghosts shall never leave
To fright thy conscience, and with thousand stings
Afflict thy soul to madness and despair.
Be patient yet, and prosper, and let fall
Thy anger on the Christians, that else
Will poison thy fair kingdom.

King. Ha! Archimagus,
Canst thou forgive me,
And send those spirits hence?

Arch. I can, great sir.—
You troubled spirits, I command you leave
The much distracted king; return, and speedily,
To sleep within the bosom of the sea,
Which the king's wrath, and your sad fates,
    assign'd you;
And as you move to your expecting monument,

The waves, again, no frown appear upon you,
But glide away in peace.

Both. } We do obey,
Great priest, and vanish.

　　　　　　　　　　　[*Exeunt End. and Fer.*

Eth. Are they gone, Fedella?
They talk of woman's wit at a dead lift;
This was above our brains ; I love him for't,
And wish myself in's arms now, to reward him ;
I should find him no ghost, o' my conscience.
But where shall we meet next?

Fed. Let us away.　　　　[*Exeunt Eth. and Fed.*

King. Art sure they are gone, Archimagus? my
　　　fears
So leave me, and religion once again
Enter my stubborn heart, which dar'd to mutiny
And quarrel with the gods! Archimagus,
Be near again, we will redeem our rashness,
By grubbing up these Christians, that begin
To infect us, and our kingdom.

Arch. This becomes you ;
And if you please to hear me, I dare promise
The speedy ruin of them all.

King. Thou'rt born
To make us happy.　How, my dear Archimagus!

Arch. This island, sir, is full of dangerous ser-
　　　pents,
Of toads, and other venemous destroyers :
I will from every province of this kingdom
Summon these killing creatures, to devour him ;
My prayer, and power of the gods, fear not,
Will do't, by whom inspired, I prophesy
Patrick's destruction.

King. I embrace my priest ;
Do this, and I'll forget my son, and die,
And smile to see this Christian's tragedy. [*Exeunt.*

ACT V. SCENE I.

A Wood.

Enter two Soldiers.

1 *Sold.* So, so! we are like to have a fine time on't. We may get more by every Christian we have the grace to catch, than by three months' pay against our natural enemies.

2 *Sold.* An their noddles be so precious, would all my kindred were Christians! I would not leave a head to wag upon a shoulder of our generation, from my mother's sucking pig at her nipple, to my great grandfather's coshering in the peas-straw.[1] How did that fellow look, whose throat we cut last?

1 *Sold.* Basely, and like a Christian; would the fellow they call Patrick had been in his place! we had been made for ever.

2 *Sold.* Now are we of the condition of some great men in office, that desire execution of the laws; not so much to correct offences, and reform the commonwealth, as to thrive by their punishment, and grow rich and fat with a lean conscience. But I have walk'd and talk'd myself a hungry; prithee open the secrets of thy knapsack; before we build any more projects, let's see what store of belly timber we have. Good! very good pagan food. Sit down, and let our stomachs confer awhile.

Enter RODAMANT, *with the bracelet on his wrist, as invisible.*

Rod. My royal love is roasted; she died of a

---

[1] *To my great grandfather's* coshering *in the peas-straw.*] A *coshering* is, I believe, a pet lamb.

burning fever; and since poison will not work upon me, I am resolved to look out the most convenient tree in this wood to hang myself; and because I will be sure to hang without molestation, or cutting down, which is a disparagement to an able and willing body, I will hang invisible, that no body may see me, and interrupt my hempen meditations. But who are these? a brace of man-killers a-munching: now I think what a long journey I am going, as far as to another world, it were not amiss to take provision along with me; when I come to the trick of hanging, I may weigh the better, and sooner be out of my pain.—Bracelet, stick to me.—By your leave, gentlemen, what's your ordinary?

1 *Sold.* Who's that?

Rod. A friend, my brace of Hungarians; one that is no soldier, but will justify he has a stomach in a just cause, and can fight tooth and nail with any flesh that opposes me.

2 *Sold.* I can see no body.

Rod. I will knock your pate, fellow in arms; and, to help you to see, open the eyes of your understanding with a wooden instrument that I have.

1 *Sold.* I see nothing but a voice; shall I strike it?

2 *Sold.* No, 'tis some spirit; take heed, and offend it not. I never knew any man strike the devil, but he put out his neck-bone or his shoulder-blade. Let him alone: it may be the ghost of some usurer that kick'd up his heels in a dear year, and died upon a surfeit of shamrocks and cheese-parings.

Enter EMERIA.

1 *Sold.* Who's this? a woman, alone!

2 *Sold.* And handsome. What makes she in this wood? we'll divide.

1 *Sold.* What, the woman?

2 *Sold.* No, I'll have her body, and thou shalt have her clothes.

Em. I know not where I am; this wood has
    lost me;
But I shall never more be worth the finding.
I was not wise to leave my father's house,
For here I may be made a prey to rapine,
Or food to cruel beasts.

2 *Sold.* No; you shall find that we are men. What think you? which of us two have you most mind to laugh and lie down withal?

Em. Protect me, some good Power! more
    ravishers?

2 *Sold.* We are soldiers, and not used to complement; be not coy, but answer.

1 *Sold.* We are but two; you may soon make a choice.

Rod. You shall find that we be three: are you so hot?

1 *Sold.* Come, humble yourself behind that tree, or—

Em. Are you a man?

2 *Sold.* Never doubt it; I have pass'd for a man in my days.   [*Rod. strikes* 2 *Sold.*

2 *Sold.* Oh my skull!

1 *Sold.* What's the matter?

Em. Where shall I hide myself?   [*Exit.*

Rod. Your comrade will expect your company in the next ditch?

2 *Sold.* Are you good at that?
        [2 *Sold. strikes the first, and Rod. both.*

1 *Sold.* What dost thou mean?

2 *Sold.* What do I mean! what dost thou mean, to beat my brains out?

1 *Sold.* I? Hold, it is some spirit, and we fight with the air.

Rod. Cannot a mare come into the ground, but you must be leaping, you stonehorses?

2 *Sold.* My skull is as tender as a mollipuff.

1 *Sold.* He has made a cullice of my sconce. Hold, dear friend.

2 *Sold.* Has the devil no more wit, than to take part against the flesh?

1 *Sold.* The devil may have a mind to her himself; let him have her.

2 *Sold.* If I come back, let me be glibb'd.

            .   [*Exeunt reeling.*

Rod. Now, lady—what, is she invisible too! Ha! well, let her shift for herself, I have tamed their concupiscence. Now to my business of hanging again.

Enter Spirit.

I do like none of these trees: the devil is at my elbow now; I do hear him whisper in mine ear, that any tree would serve, if I would but give my mind to't. Let me consider; what shall I get by hanging of myself? how!—it will be to no purpose, a halter will be but cast away. By your leave.— I would not have you much out of the way, because here are trees that other men may hold convenient.—Oh, my wrist! 'tis a spirit.—Sweet devil, you shall have it; the bracelet is at your service. [*unclasps the bracelet, which the Spirit takes, and exit.*]—Have I all my fingers? a pox on his fangs! Now, o' my conscience, I am visible again; if the soldiers should meet with me now, whom I have pounded, what case were I in! I feel a distillation, and would be heartily beaten to save my life.—

Re-enter EMERIA, *with* CONALLUS.

Here's one, for aught I know, may be as dangerous. A pox of despair, that brought me hither to choose

my gallows! would I were at home in an embroi-
dered clout!—I'll sneak this way.   [*Exit.*

Em. I am no ghost, but the same lost Emeria,
My lord, you left me.

Con. Did not the flames devour thee?

Em. I felt no flame, but that which my revenge
Did light me to, for my abused honour.

Con. Oh, say that word again; art thou re-
venged
Upon thy ravisher? it was a god,
Thou told'st me.   ·

Em. But he found the way to death;
And when I name him, you will either not
Believe me, or compassion of his wounds
Will make you print as many in my breast:
He was——

Con. Say, fear not, wrong'd Emeria.
Can any heart find compassion for his death,
That murder'd the sweet peace of thy chaste
bosom?
Oh, never; I shall bless that resolute hand
That was so just, so pious; and when thou hast
Assur'd, that he which play'd the satyr with thee,
Is out o' the world, and kill'd sufficiently,
(For he that robb'd thee hath deserv'd to die,
To the extent of his wide sin,) I'll kiss,
And take thee in mine arms, Emeria,
And lay thee up as precious to my love,
As when our vows met, and our yielding bosoms
Were witness to the contract of our hearts.

Em. It was your brother Corybreus, sir:
That name unties your promise.

Con. Ha! my brother!
Sweet, let me pause a little, I am lost else.

Em. I did not well to enlarge his sorrow thus:
Though I can hope no comfort in this world,
He might live happy, if I did not kill him,
With heaping grief on grief thus.

Con. He is slain then?

Em. If you will, sir, revenge his death, you must
Point your wrath here, and I will thank you for't,
Though you should be a day in killing me,
I should live so much longer to forgive you.
This weak hand did not tremble when it kill'd him,
And it came timely to prevent, I fear,
The second part of horror he had meant
To act upon me.

Con. Would he had took my life,
When he assail'd thy chastity, so thou
Hadst been preserv'd! I cannot help all this.
Did it not grieve thee he deserv'd to die, ha?

Em. I took no joy, sir, in his tragedy.

Con. That done, thou fled'st.

Em. I left my father's house,
And found no weight hung on my feet for giving
His lust the bloody recompense.

Con. Thou art happy:
The gods directed thee to fly, Emeria,
Thou hadst been lost else, with my brother's ashes,
And my dear mother, whom the hungry flames
Devour'd, soon after thy departure.

Em. How!

Con. I know not by what malice, or misfortune,
Thy father's house was burn'd, and in it he
Did meet his funeral fire too.—Ha! Emeria!

Enter St. Patrick, Queen, *and* Bard.

Bard. Your company's fair, but I'll leave you
in a wood. I could like your religion well; but
those rules of fasting, prayer, and so much penance,
will hardly fit my constitution.

St. P. 'Tis nothing, to win heaven.

Bard. But you do not consider that I shall lose
my pension, my pension from the king; there's a
business!

Queen. Do not I leave more?

Bard. I confess it, and you will get less by the bargain; but you, that have been used to hunger, and nothing to live upon, may make the better shift. The less you eat, you say, will make the soul fat; but I have a body will not be used so: I must drink, and go warm, and make much of my voice, I cannot do good upon water and sallads. Keep your diet-drink to yourselves, I am a kind of foolish courtier, Patrick; with us, wine and women are provocatives; long tables and short graces are physical, and in fashion. —I'll take my leave, madam; no Christian yet, as the world goes; perhaps hereafter, when my voice is aweary of me, I may grow weary of the world, and stoop to your ordinary, say my prayers, and think how to die, when my living is taken from me; in the mean time— [*Sings.*

> *I neither will lend nor borrow,*
> *Old age will be here to-morrow;*
> *This pleasure we are made for,*
> *When death comes all is paid for:*
> > *No matter what's the bill of fare,*
> > *I'll take my cup, I'll take no care.*

> *Be wise, and say you had warning,*
> *To laugh is better than learning;*
> *To wear no clothes, not neat is;*
> *But hunger is good where meat is:*
> > *Give me wine, give me a wench,*
> > *And let her parrot talk in French.*

> *It is a match worth the making.*
> *To keep the merry-thought waking;*
> *A song is better than fasting,*
> *And sorrow's not worth the tasting:*
> > *Then keep your brain light as you can,*
> > *An ounce of care will kill a man.*

And so I take my leave. [*Exit.*

Con. Ha! do I see the queen, Emeria?

St. P. Alas, poor bard, the flatteries of this
 world
Have chain'd his sense: thus many self-loving
 natures,
Prison'd in mists and errors, cannot see
The way abroad that leads to happiness,
Or truth, whose beamy hand should guide us in it.
What a poor value do men set of heaven!
Heaven, the perfection of all that can
Be said, or thought, riches, delight, or harmony,
Health, beauty, and all these not subject to
The waste of time, but in their height eternal,
Lost for a pension, or poor spot of earth,
Favour of greatness, or an hour's faint pleasure:
As men, in scorn of a true flame that's near,
Should run to light their taper at a glow-worm.

Con. 'Tis she! and the good bishop Patrick
 with her.

St. P. Madam, the prince Conallus.

Con. Oh, let me kneel to you, and then to heaven,
That hath preserv'd you still to be my mother,
For I believe you are alive; the fire
Hath not defaced this monument of sweetness.

Queen. My blessing, and my prayers be still my
 child's.
It was the goodness, son, of holy Patrick,
That rescued me from those impris'ning flames
You speak of; his good angel was our conduct.

Con. To him that can dispense such blessings,
 mother,
I must owe duty, and thus kneeling, pay it:
May angels still be near you!

St. P. Rise, Conallus;
My benediction on thee; be but what
Thy mother is, a Christian, and a guard
Of angels shall attend thee too: the fire
We walk'd upon secure, and, which is greater,

'Scap'd the immortal flames, in which black souls,
After their ill-spent lives, are bound to suffer.
   Con. Sir, you shall steer me, and my mother's
       blest
Example will become my imitation :
But there's a piece of silent misery
Is worth your comfort, mother, and his counsel ;
She is, I dare not name how much dishonour'd,
And should have been the partner of my bosom,
Had not a cruel man forbid my happiness,
And on that fair and innocent table pour'd
Poison, above the dragon's blood, or viper's.
   Em. My humblest duty, madam.
   St. P. Dichu's cell
Is not far off; please you attend the queen ;
We are bent thither.
   Con. Yes; and as we walk,
I'll tell you a sad story of my brother,
And this poor virgin.
   St. P. Come, I'll lead the way.
   Queen. With such a guide we cannot fear to
    stray.   [*Exeunt.*

SCENE II.

Another Part of the Same.

Enter FEROCHUS *and* ENDARIUS, *in the same state
in which they quitted the Temple.*

   Fer. Where are we yet, Endarius ?
   End. I cannot
Inform you more, than that we are in the wood still.
   Fer. And we are lost; our fear to die i' the sight
Of men hath brought us hither with our blood,
To quench the thirst of wolves ; or, worse, to starve.

End. We are in no fear to be apprehended,
Where none inhabit.

Fer. Now that lust is punish'd
Which fed our hope, if we had staid i' the temple,
To have polluted it with foul embraces.
How weariness, with travel, and some fasting,
Will tame the flesh!

End. Stay, here's a cave.

Fer. Take heed,
It may be a lion or a fierce wolf's den.
How nature trembles at the thought of death,
Though it be press'd down with the weight of life!

End. I dare not enter ; a new fear invades me.

Fer. The worst is welcome ; with our clamour
    rouze
Whatever doth inhabit here :—[*Aloud.*] Or man,
Or beast appear, if any such dwell in
This cave!—We can meet charity or death.

Enter DICHU *in the dress of a hermit.*

Dic. What voice with so much passion calls me
    forth?
Ha! be my protection, good heaven!
My sons, my murder'd sons, with ghastly looks,
And bruised limbs! Why do you come to me thus,
To fright my wither'd eyes? 'Las! I was innocent ;
It was the king, not I, commanded your
Untimely death. I have wept for ye, boys,
And constantly, before the sun awak'd,
When the cold dew-drops fell upon the ground,
As if the morn were discontented too,
My naked feet o'er many a rugged stone
Have walk'd, to drop my tears into the seas,
For your sad memories.

Fer. We are no spirits, but your living sons,
Preserv'd without the knowledge of the king,
By Archimagus, till a new misfortune

Compell'd us hither, to meet death, we fear,
In want of food.

Dic. Are ye alive?   Come in,
It is no time to be inquisitive ;
My blessing, I have something to refresh you,
Coarse fare, but such as will keep out sad famine.
Humble yourselves and enter,[1] my poor boys ;
You'll wonder at the change ; but we to heaven
Do climb, with loads upon our shoulders born,
Nor must we tread on roses, but on thorn.

[*Exeunt.*

SCENE III.

In front of Dichu's *Cell.*

Enter St. PATRICK, Queen, CONALLUS, *and* EMERIA.

St. P. Now we approach the hermit Dichu's
cell.—
Are you not weary, madam?

Queen. Not yet, father,
In such religious company.

St. P. You were not
Used to this travel.—How does my new son?
And sweet Emeria?

Con. I am blest on all sides.

Em. You have quieted the tempest in my soul,
And in this holy peace I must be happy.

St. P. You will be spouse to an eternal bride-
groom,
And lay the sweet foundation of a rule,
That after ages, with devotion,
Shall praise and follow.—You are, sir, reserv'd
To bless this kingdom with your pious govern-
ment:

---

[1] Humble *yourselves and enter.*] i. e. stoop. Shirley appears to have the cave of Bellarius in view. See *Cymbeline.*

Your crown shall flourish, and your blood possess
The throne you shall leave glorious : this nation
Shall in a fair succession thrive, and grow
Up the world's académy, and disperse,
As the rich spring of human and divine
Knowledge, clear streams to water foreign king-
      doms ;
Which shall be proud to owe what they possess
In learning, to this great all-nursing island.
   Con May we be worthy of this prophecy !
   St. P. Discourse hath made the way less tedious.
We have reach'd the cell already, which is much
Too narrow to contain us ; but beneath
These trees, upon their cool and pleasing shades,
You may sit down ; I'll call upon my convert.—
Dichu, my penitent, come forth, I pray,
And entertain some guests I have brought hither,
That deserve welcome.

Enter DICHU.

   Dic. I obey that voice.
   St. P. The queen, and prince, and Milcho's vir-
      tuous daughter,
Gain'd to our holy faith.
   Dic. Let my knee speak
My duty, though I want words for my joy ;
Ten thousand welcomes ! I have guests within too,
You'll wonder to salute ; my sons, not dead,
As we supposed ; by heavenly providence,
I hope, reserved to be made blest by you.
They are here.—

Enter FEROCHUS *and* ENDARIUS.

Your duties to the queen and prince,
Then to this man, next to our Great Preserver,
The patron of us all.
   St. P. A happy meeting !

75

I must rejoice to see you safe, and here;
But tell us by what strange means, all this while,
You have been preserv'd?   Sit down. [*Soft music*.
  Con. What music's this?
  Queen. 'Tis heavenly.
  St. P. And a preface to some message,
Or will of heaven.   Be silent, and attend it.
                    [*They all sleep but St. P.*
Such harmony as this did wait upon
My angel Victor, when he first appear'd,
And did reveal a treasure under ground,
With which I bought my freedom, when I kept
Unhappy Milcho's swine. Heaven's will be done.—
What, all asleep already? holy dreams
Possess your fancy!—I can [wake] no longer.
                    [*Sleeps.*

Enter VICTOR, *and other Angels.*

SONG.

  Vict. Down from the skies,
    Commanded by the Power that ties
      The world and nature in a chain,
    We come, we come, a glorious train,
      To wait on thee,
    And make thy person danger-free:
      Hark, whilst we sing,
    And keep time with our golden wing,
    To shew how earth and heaven agree,
    What echo rises to our harmony!

  Vict. Holy Patrick, sleep in peace,
Whilst I, thy guardian, with these
My fellow angels, wait on thee,
For thy defence : a troop, I see,
Of serpents, vipers, and whate'er
Doth carry killing poison, here
Summon'd by art, and power of hell ;
But thou shalt soon their fury quell,
                    G g 2

And by the strength of thy command,
These creatures shall forsake the land,
And creep into the sea; no more
To live upon the Irish shore.

Once more then.

SONG.

<blockquote>

Patrick, sleep; oh, sleep awhile,
And wake the patron of this isle!
</blockquote>

[Exeunt Vict. and Angels

Enter King, ARCHIMAGUS, *and* Magicians.

Arch. Your person shall be safe; fear not, great
    sir,
I have directed all their stings, and poison.
See where he sleeps; if he escape this danger,
Let my life, with some horrid circumstance,
End in this place, and carry all your curses.

Serpents, &c. creep in.

What think you of these creeping executioners!
Do they not move, as if they knew their errand?
    King. My queen! my son, Conallus! Dichu!
    ha!
And the still-wand'ring ghosts of his two sons!
    Arch. They are alive, sir.
    King. Ha! who durst abuse us?
    1 *Mag.* Will you not have compassion of the
    queen,
And the prince, sir?
    King. How met they to converse?
    Arch. They are all Christians.
    King. Let the serpents then
Feed upon all, my powerful Archimagus.
    St. P. [*waking.*]—In vain is all your malice, art,
    and power

77

Against their lives, whom the great hand of heaven
Deigns to protect. Like wolves, you undertake
A quarrel with the moon, and waste your anger;
Nay, all the shafts your wrath directeth hither,
Are shot against a brazen arch, whose vault
Impenetrable sends the arrows back,
To print just wounds on your own guilty heads.
These serpents (tame at first and innocent,
Until man's great revolt from grace releas'd
Their duty of creation) you have brought,
And arm'd against my life ; all these can I
Approach, and without trembling, walk upon ;
Play with their stings, which, though to me not
   dangerous,
I could, to your destruction, turn upon
Yourselves, and punish with too late repentance.
But you shall live ; and what your malice meant
My ruin, I will turn to all your safeties,
And you shall witness. — Hence, you frightful
  monsters !
Go hide, and bury your deformed heads
For ever in the sea ! from this time be
This island free from beasts of venemous natures.
The shepherd shall not be afraid hereafter
To trust his eyes with sleep upon the hills ;
The traveller shall [from hence] have no suspicion,
Or fear, to measure with his wearied limbs
The silent shades ; but walk through every brake,
Without more guard than his own innocence.
The very earth and wood shall have this blessing,
(Above what other christian nations boast,)
Although transported where these serpents live
And multiply, one touch shall soon destroy them.
      [*The reptiles creep away.*
 King. See how they all obey him, Archimagus !
 Arch. Confusion ! all my art is trampled on.
Can neither man, nor beast, nor devil hurt him?
Support me, fellow priests ; I sink, I feel

The ground bend with my weight upon it.   Ha !
The earth is loose in the foundation,
And something heavy as the world doth hang
Upon my feet, and weigh me to the centre.
A fire, a dreadful fire is underneath me,
And all those fiends, that were my servants here,
Look like tormentors, and all seem to strive
Who first shall catch my falling flesh upon
Their burning pikes.   There is a Power above
Our gods, I see too late.   I fall ! I fall !
And in my last despair, I curse you all.   [*Sinks.*

   King. Patrick, the king will kneel to thee.
   St. P. Oh, rise,
And pay to heaven that duty.
   King. Canst forgive ?
Let me embrace you all, and freely give,
What I desire from this good man, a pardon.
Thou shalt no more suspect me, but possess
All thy desires.— The ground is shut again :
Where now is Archimagus '—How I shake,
And court this Christian, out of fear, not love !—
Once more visit our palace, holy father.—
The story of your sons, and what concerns
Your escape, madam, we will know hereafter :
I' the mean time be secure.

   End.⎱
   Fer.⎰ We are your creatures.

   Omnes. Our prayers and duty.
   St. P. I suspect him still ;
But fear not, our good angels still are near us :
Death at the last can but untie our frailty.
'Twere happy for our holy faith to bleed,
The blood of martyrs is the church's seed.
                              [*Exeunt.*

ST. PATRICK FOR IRELAND.

EPILOGUE.

Howe'er the dice run, gentlemen, I am
The last man borne still at the Irish game.[1]
What say you to the Epilogue? may I stay,
And boldly ask your verdict of the play?
I would report the sunshine on your brow,
And the soft language of the D'ye 't allow?
Our labour and your story, native known,
It is but justice to affect your own;
Yet this is but a part of what our muse
Intends, if the first birth you nobly use:
Then give us your free votes, and let us style
You patrons of the play, Him of the isle.

[1] *The* Irish game.] A complicated kind of *back-gammon.* It was once very popular, and is noticed by most of our old dramatists. Instructions for playing it are given in the *Complete Gentleman.*

Also from Benediction Books ...

Wandering Between Two Worlds: Essays on Faith and Art
Anita Mathias
Benediction Books, 2007
152 pages
ISBN: 0955373700

Available from www.amazon.com, www.amazon.co.uk
www.wanderingbetweentwoworlds.com

In these wide-ranging lyrical essays, Anita Mathias writes, in lush, lovely prose, of her naughty Catholic childhood in Jamshedpur, India; her large, eccentric family in Mangalore, a sea-coast town converted by the Portuguese in the sixteenth century; her rebellion and atheism as a teenager in her Himalayan boarding school, run by German missionary nuns, St. Mary's Convent, Nainital; and her abrupt religious conversion after which she entered Mother Teresa's convent in Calcutta as a novice. Later rich, elegant essays explore the dualities of her life as a writer, mother, and Christian in the United States-- Domesticity and Art, Writing and Prayer, and the experience of being "an alien and stranger" as an immigrant in America, sensing the need for roots.

About the Author

Anita Mathias was born in India, has a B.A. and M.A. in English from Somerville College, Oxford University and an M.A. in Creative Writing from the Ohio State University. Her essays have been published in The Washington Post, The London Magazine, The Virginia Quarterly Review, Commonweal, Notre Dame Magazine, America, The Christian Century, Religion Online, The Southwest Review, Contemporary Literary Criticism, New Letters, The Journal, and two of HarperSanFrancisco's The Best Spiritual Writing anthologies. Her non-fiction has won fellowships from The National Endowment for the Arts; The Minnesota State Arts Board; The Jerome Foundation, The Vermont Studio Center; The Virginia Centre for the Creative Arts, and the First Prize for the Best General Interest Article from the Catholic Press Association of the United States and Canada. Anita has taught Creative Writing at the College of William and Mary, and now lives and writes in Oxford, England.

Religio Medici, Hydriotaphia, Letter to a Friend, Thomas Browne

Pseudodoxia Epidemica: Or, Enquiries into Commonly Presumed Truths, Thomas Browne

The Maid's Tragedy, Beaumont and Fletcher

The Custom of the Country, Beaumont and Fletcher

Philaster Or Love Lies a Bleeding, Beaumont and Fletcher

A Treatise of Fishing with an Angle,   Dame Juliana Berners.

Pamphilia to Amphilanthus, Lady Mary Wroth

The Compleat Angler, Izaak Walton

The Magnetic Lady, Ben Jonson

Every Man Out of His Humour, Ben Jonson

The Masque of Blacknesse. The Masque of Beauty,. Ben Jonson

The Life of St. Thomas More, William Roper

Pendennis, William Makepeace Thackeray

Salmacis and Hermaphroditus attributed to Francis Beaumont

Friar Bacon and Friar Bungay Robert Greene

Holy Wisdom, Augustine Baker

The Jew of Malta and the Massacre at Paris, Christopher Marlowe

Tamburlaine the Great, Parts 1 & 2 AND Massacre at Paris, Christopher Marlowe

All Ovids Elegies, Lucans First Booke, Dido Queene of Carthage, Hero and Leander, Christopher Marlowe

The Titan, Theodore Dreiser

Trilogy of Desire: "The Financier" , "The Titan" and "The Stoic", Theodore Dreiser

Scapegoats of the Empire: The true story of the Bushveldt Carbineers, George Witton

All Hallows' Eve, Charles Williams

Descent into Hell, Charles Williams

My Apprenticeship: Volumes I and II, Beatrice Webb

Last and First Men / Star Maker, Olaf Stapledon

Darkness and the Light, Olaf Stapledon

The Worst Journey in the World, Apsley Cherry-Garrard

The Schoole of Abuse, Containing a Pleasaunt Invective Against Poets, Pipers, Plaiers, Iesters and Such Like Catepillers of the Commonwelth, Stephen Gosson

Russia in the Shadows, H. G. Wells

Wild Swans at Coole, W. B. Yeats

A hundreth good pointes of husbandrie, Thomas Tusser

The Collected Works of Nathanael West: "The Day of the Locust", "The Dream Life of Balso Snell", "Miss Lonelyhearts", "A Cool Million", Nathanael West

Miss Lonelyhearts & The Day of the Locust, Nathaniel West

The Worst Journey in the World, Apsley Cherry-Garrard

Scott's Last Expedition, V1, R. F. Scott

The Herries Chronicle: Rogue Herries, Judith Paris, The Fortress and Vanessa, Hugh Walpole

Rogue Herries, Hugh Walpole

Judith Paris, Hugh Walpole

The Fortress, Hugh Walpole

Vanessa, Hugh Walpole

The Dream of Gerontius, John Henry Newman

The Brother of Daphne, Dornford Yates

The Poetry of Architecture: Or the Architecture of the Nations of Europe Considered in Its Association with Natural Scenery and National Character, John Ruskin

The Downfall of Robert Earl of Huntington, Anthony Munday

Clayhanger, Arnold Bennett

South: The Story of Shackleton's Last Expedition 1914-1917, Sir Ernest Shackketon

The Bishop and Other Stories, Anton Chekov

Greene's Groatsworth of Wit: Bought With a Million of Repentance, Robert Greene

Beau Sabreur, Percival Christopher Wren

The Hekatompathia, or Passionate Centurie of Love, Thomas Watson

The Road to Wigan Pier, George Orwell

The Art of Rhetoric, Thomas Wilson

Stepping Heavenward, Elizabeth Prentiss

Barker's Delight, or The Art of Angling, Thomas Barker

The Napoleon of Notting Hill, G.K. Chesterton

The Douay-Rheims Bible (The Challoner Revision)

Endimion - The Man in the Moone, John Lyly

Gallathea and Midas, Lyly, John

Manners, Custom and Dress During the Middle Ages and During the Renaissance Period, Paul Lacroix

Obedience of a Christian Man, William Tyndale

St. Patrick for Ireland, James Shirley

The Wrongs of Woman; Or Maria/Memoirs of the Author of a Vindication of the Rights of Woman, Mary Wollstonecraft and William Godwin

and many others

Tell us what you would love to see in print again, at affordable prices!
Email: **benedictionbooks@btinternet.com**

Printed in France by Amazon
Brétigny-sur-Orge, FR